OTHER BOOKS BY NEAL SHUSTERMAN

YOUNG ADULT NOVELS:

Dissidents
Speeding Bullet
What Daddy Did
The Eyes of Kid Midas
The Dark Side of Nowhere
Downsiders
Full Tilt
The Shadow Club Rising

STORY COLLECTIONS:

Kid Heroes
Darkness Creeping
Darkness Creeping II
MindQuakes
MindStorms
MindTwisters
MindBenders

NOVELS FOR OLDER READERS:

The Star Shard Trilogy:
Scorpion Shards
Thief of Souls
Shattered Sky

Visit the author's Web site at:
WWW.STORYMAN.COM

THE
SHADOW
CLUB

NEAL SHUSTERMAN

Dutton Children's Books ▫ *NEW YORK*

Library of Congress Cataloging-in-Publication Data
Shusterman, Neal.
The Shadow Club / by Neal Shusterman.
p. cm.
Originally published: Boston: Little, Brown, 1988.
Sequel: Shadow club rising.
Summary: When a junior high school boy and his friends decide to form a club of "second bests" and play anonymous tricks on each other's archrivals, the harmless pranks escalate until they become life-threatening.   ISBN 0-525-46833-1
[1. Clubs—Fiction. 2. Practical jokes—Fiction. 3. Schools—Fiction.] I. Title.
PZ7.S55987   Sh   2002   [Fic]—dc21   2001047150

Originally published 1988 by Little, Brown and Company, Boston.
This edition published in the United States 2002 by Dutton Children's Books,
a division of Penguin Putnam Books for Young Readers
345 Hudson Street, New York, New York 10014
www.penguinputnam.com

Designed by Heather Wood • Printed in USA • Reissued Edition
10   9   8   7   6   5   4   3   2   1

For my parents,
in whose eyes I was never second best,
and for Elaine,
with whom I've come full circle

THE
SHADOW
CLUB

Prologue

I **SUPPOSE YOU** want to know all about us, don't you? All the nasty, horrible details about the vicious things we did. How we planned the accidents, how we plotted against everyone who got in our way. That's what you want to hear, isn't it?

Well, it wasn't like that—not to us anyway—not at first. Things just got carried away, that's all. We were all good kids—I mean *really* good kids. Not a single kid in the Shadow Club had ever done anything bad and there wasn't a single delinquent in the bunch. Not at first.

I still don't know how it all happened. We just lost control, ya know—too many bad feelings have a way of spinning together into one killer tornado, and none of us in the Shadow Club knew how to stop it, or for that matter, where it was going.

I haven't told anyone the whole story yet. I don't like to talk about it, because it scares me. I get nightmares. When I was little, I got nightmares about werewolves, or dumb things like that. Now I get nightmares about myself. And since it happened, I've been catching other kids looking at me funny, like I'm a different person now, like I'm that monster I dream about. But it's not true! And I don't know how to prove to them that *I'm still me!* I'm just a whole lot smarter now, that's all.

Like I said, I haven't told anyone, but I can't keep it in anymore. If I do, I'll go crazy.

So listen closely. I'll tell you all there is to know about the Shadow Club . . . but you have to promise you won't hate me when I'm done.

I'll begin long before any of the bad stuff happened, before I spied on Tyson McGaw—even before the first meeting. Way back when that tornado wasn't even a breeze, just a bunch of thoughts kept secretly in the back of our minds, thoughts we were sure no one else could understand.

It all started that day in the graveyard. . . .

Stupid-Talk

IT **WAS THE** strangest place for anyone to have a wedding, and whoever came up with the idea of having weddings there must have had a very sick mind. This town has to be the only town in the history of the world that has weddings in a cemetery.

Anyway, it was the first day of September, and we all stood there in the rose garden at the very edge of Shady Bluff Memorial Park, sipping punch from tiny cups and stuffing our faces with little cheese hors d'oeuvres, waiting for the wedding to start. Cheryl's mom was getting married.

Cheryl had been nervously chewing the lip of her cup until there was none of it left, and checking to see if her hair was still in place. She had good reason to be nervous, since it *was* her mother's wedding, and she was about to have a new father, but that wasn't the only reason she was nervous.

"I just know they're going to ask me to sing," Cheryl mumbled under her breath.

"Huh?" said Randall, her younger brother.

"Sing. They're going to ask me to sing."

"Don't be dumb," he said. "People don't sing in cemeteries." (Which was a good point.)

"No, I mean later," said Cheryl, "at the house, during the party. They always ask me to sing."

Randall rolled his eyeballs so far back you could almost hear them turning in his head. "Like when?"

Cheryl thought for a moment, then a smirk spread over her face.

"Like at *your* birthday party!" she said triumphantly. She looked at me, but I knew better than to stick my nose in this one. My nose has been whacked too many times for being where it never should have been in the first place. This was *their* argument.

"Yeah, well guess what?" said Randall, "I got news for you—nobody asked you. You got up there and sang anyway, all on your lonesome."

"That's not true," said Cheryl. "Somebody asked me."

"Who?"

"I don't remember who, that doesn't matter. The point is that I was asked . . . and as I recall, everyone clapped."

"They clapped because I blew out the candles," said Randall.

"Well, that, too . . . but they liked the way I led 'Happy Birthday.' I kept them all in tune."

"You were louder than everyone else, you mean—and

you didn't have to stand on a chair. That was embarrassing."

"Someone has to lead!" demanded Cheryl. "It's like the national anthem at a ball game. Someone has to lead it, or everyone sings at the wrong time, out of tune, and it sounds lousy!"

It was about this time that I forced my ears closed and tuned the two of them out. True, Cheryl and Randall were my friends, but there's only so much stupid-talk a human brain can listen to—and when Cheryl and Randall got started, they could stupid-talk each other till their mouths wore out. I turned off my brain whenever my parents did it, and I turned off my brain whenever my friends did it.

I was closer friends with Cheryl than I was with Randall. In fact, you could say that Cheryl was my best friend. She had been my best friend all of my life, or as far back as I could remember; back to the days when it was all right for little boys to play with little girls, because we didn't really know the difference, and through the time when everyone would make fun of us because boys were supposed to do boys' things with boys, and girls were supposed to do girls' things with girls. Now, no one much bothered us, because at four-teen everyone has more sense. Besides, people envied us, be-cause everyone was so sure we were a lot more than we really were, if you know what I mean. Other kids always think that kind of thing if you're friends with a girl.

Anyway, neither Cheryl nor Randall knew when to shut

up, or when to give up, since they were always so convinced that they were right. They argued like lawyers, which is something they both got from their mother, who *is* a lawyer. This time, however, I knew for a fact that Randall was right. No one had asked Cheryl to sing at that party. The only person that was asked to sing was Cheryl's cousin Rebecca, and luckily, Cheryl was out back when it happened, or else she would have been in an evil mood for the rest of the day. Cheryl hated Rebecca about as much as I hated Austin Pace . . . but I'll leave that for later.

"You just watch," said Cheryl. "Mom will come over to me and ask me to sing when she and Paul have their first dance. I'll bet you."

"You're on," said Randall. "I'd bet you money, but I wouldn't want to make you feel *too* bad."

"Fine. It's settled then," I said, just to shut them up. "The winner gets no money, but will get to hang their victory over the other person's head for the rest of their life, all right?"

"Fine," they both said.

"Good. Now both of you shut up, because it looks like they're going to start."

In a few minutes Randall and Cheryl left to join the bridal party, which would come down the aisle along with the bride. My parents found me and we went to sit in the rows of chairs by the little vine-covered gazebo in which the wedding would take place.

The air was still warm that day, as if it had forgotten autumn was coming pretty soon—but the trees remembered. You could tell that they were just about ready to start turning colors. It was a nice day for a wedding.

Cheryl came down the aisle with the rest of the bridesmaids. I knew she hated all that makeup and hair spray, but I have to admit, I'd never seen her look so beautiful—even more beautiful than her mother did in her wedding dress. Of course I couldn't tell Cheryl that; she tended to punch people who told her she looked beautiful.

As the ceremony went on, I saw Cheryl's cousin Rebecca on the other side of the aisle. She sat there like a little princess, all four feet of her, pretending to be the cutest thing on earth, like she was taking Shirley Temple lessons or something. Even just sitting, you could sense that air about her. Like she was the one in Cheryl's family that everyone adored, and she knew it. I could see why Cheryl resented her; who wouldn't? All that pretend sweetness all rolled up into one tiny body. What made it even more irksome for Cheryl was that next week Rebecca would make her grand entrance into our junior high, and would, as always, set out to top anything Cheryl had ever done.

Well, the wedding went fine, and so did the first half of the party back in Cheryl's backyard. It was when the band started its second set that things started to change.

It seemed that Cheryl was having such a great time,

dancing and jabbering at anyone who had an ear, that she forgot all about her little bet with Randall back in the old graveyard rose garden. It could have gone forgotten, and no one, not even Randall, would have cared . . . but something happened.

Cheryl and I were dancing quite a lot, since we both liked to dance, and were tiring ourselves out, when the lead singer ended the song and began talking.

"How we doin' out there?" he asked the guests. A few people mumbled "Good." "Great!" said the lead singer. "Now, we have a very special request. I understand there is a young lady here who is quite a singer . . ."

"I knew it!" said Cheryl, and she cleared her throat half a dozen times.

". . . and we have a very special request from the bride for her to come up here and give us a song . . ." continued the singer.

Cheryl cracked her knuckles, which made me wince, and cleared her throat again. Randall, from across the yard, caught her gaze, amazed that his sister was actually going to win.

". . . so, maybe if we give her a great big hand," continued the singer, "she'll come on up and sing for us!"

Cheryl bit her lip and leaned forward, sure that the eyes of the whole world were looking at her.

The singer put on a big smile. "Let's hear it for . . . Rebecca!"

Cheryl took one step forward and then it hit her. You could almost hear her jaw drop open. People began to applaud, and Randall began to laugh. Then he turned to Cheryl, scratched his head, and gave her his best monkey impersonation. Cheryl ignored him and turned to me. For a split second she had that look in her eye that you only see in movies about people possessed by the devil, but the look faded. She sighed and said, "Well, that just figures, doesn't it?"

"You should go up there and sing with her," I said.

"Nope," said Cheryl, "I wasn't asked. Darned if I'm gonna make a fool of myself like she's going to."

Rebecca stepped onto the patio, where the band was. She was all of twelve, but looked more like she was nine. Even younger with the cutesy dress she was wearing. Shirley Temple lessons.

The band began to play the requested song, and Rebecca began to pretend she was a rock star. Personally, I thought that Cheryl sang a little bit better, but what do I know?

Needless to say, Cheryl and I didn't dance. We sat down at a table. I could feel all the food and dancing already taking its toll on my stomach. Or maybe it was just the song.

"You know, the second-best never get any credit," said Cheryl. "Not even from their parents."

"You're not second-best," I offered.

"I am. They're right, she does sing better than me." Cheryl played with a fork on somebody else's dessert plate that had been left there when the somebody else had gotten up to dance. "You know what really ticks me off," said Cheryl, "is that singing is the thing I do best. I mean, if there was anything else that I could really do well, it wouldn't be so bad, but I can't. All I can really do is sing, you know?"

She tapped the icing-covered fork a few times, and then a smile appeared on her face. "I wish we were back in the cemetery," she said.

"Why?"

"Because if we were, sweet-little-Becky would never make it out of there alive!" And then she laughed that sinister *Mwwaah-ha-haah* laugh reserved for mad scientists.

"Ahh, you wouldn't hurt her and you know it!" I said.

"Yeah, but I can have lots of fun pretending, can't I?" She put down the fork and thought for a moment. "Let's see . . . what could we do? We could . . . uh . . . wire her braces shut so she couldn't sing—only hum!"

"Pretty good," I said, smiling. "How about putting hydrochloric acid in her punch?"

"No, no, no," said Cheryl, getting excited. "We'll get an enormous cork, cover it with Super Glue, and drop it in the barrel on Halloween when it's her turn to bob for apples."

I laughed. "Wait . . . umm . . . We scare her so much that she screams so loud she could never sing again! No mess, no evidence!"

"What genius!" Cheryl laughed. "What genius! How

about we send her in for a tonsillectomy, but we write on her chart to remove her vocal cords instead!"

"Echhh! You're sick, Cheryl."

"Look who's talking, Jared!"

We both laughed for a while, then looked over at Little Miss Golden Throat, holding the microphone like she was born with it in her hands, and we laughed some more.

"Don't you ever imagine doing nasty things to the people that really tick you off like that?" she asked. That was a question I didn't even have to think about.

"Like every day," I said.

"And I'll bet I know just who it is!"

She giggled. She knew who, all right. It didn't take much thinking to figure out. It was Austin Pace. My very good friend Austin Pace. My buddy. My teammate. My pal. It's kind of a weird feeling to hate a friend. You don't know whether to go and have fun together, or to punch him out. Not that I would ever punch Austin out. It's just that sometimes you like to think about it, that's all. Kind of like throwing darts at someone's picture.

The song ended and everyone applauded. Then the lead singer got on the microphone again and said, "Let's hear it for Rebecca!" The applause got louder. Cheryl grimaced.

"You wanna hear another one?" asked the lead singer. Cheryl looked at me with that please-God-no expression on her face, but the applause got louder. Rebecca mumbled something to the band, they nodded and started up again—another big dance number. Rebecca began to bounce around again, and strut across the stage, all proud, sticking her chest out (which was wishful thinking on her part, if you know what I mean). Then Cheryl and I watched some old relative toss flowers at Rebecca from the floral centerpieces on the tables, and she put one behind her ear.

"I think I'm going to be sick," said Cheryl as we watched a scene that was beginning to resemble a freak show.

Austin
Pace

IN OUR TOWN, high school doesn't start in ninth grade. A hundred years ago, some founding father decided that seventh through ninth grades belonged in junior high school, and no one's bothered to change it since. It was the first day of the last year of junior high, and Austin was already at it. He was even early that morning, jogging around the track. Coach Shuler hadn't even come in yet and there was Austin, in last year's gym shorts, running in circles for the whole world to see. I am certain he was doing it for that reason—so the whole school could walk by and say, "Wow, Austin's really dedicated, isn't he?"

Well, I was dedicated, too, but I didn't flaunt it in public.

Austin is good at a large number of things. Good enough for people to notice, but not enough to be labeled "a brain," or "a jock," or "a nerd," or anything. In short, he's what every kid wants to be, or at least what I always wanted to be. He is, in his own way, perfection on two feet, and he knows it. I hated him. He didn't know that. To him I was just one of his many friends. If he had been a year or two older than me, he might have been someone I looked up to, can you believe that? He loves it when younger kids look up to him. I'm not younger, though; I'm three months older than him. And he never really treated me like a friend—or even like an equal. He kind of treated me like a worm—or at least tried to make me feel like one.

I used to think it was because I was the one who started up that now infamous nickname that still plagued his existence:

L'Austin Space.

The name stuck to him like Velcro, and he could never peel it off. Yeah, I used to think that was why he treated me like he did, but that wasn't it. It ran deeper and stronger than that. You see, unlike everyone else, I was the only one who came close to being a threat to him.

Like I said, Austin's good in everything, but there was only one thing that he was out-and-out great at. He could run. As a kid everyone knew he was fast. He beat everyone he ever challenged—even kids older than him—for as long as I can remember.

And, for as long as I can remember, I was second fastest; always the second-best runner. It wouldn't have been so bad being second-best, but you see, it was what I did best out of everything—just like Cheryl and her singing. I wasn't outstanding in any of my classes, and I wasn't the most popular guy in school. Whatever it was, I was always somewhere in the middle. I was the guy you would never notice. They used to call me the Generic Kid when I was ten, because at day camp none of the counselors could remember my name. I just didn't stand out.

But I could run, and when you're a fast runner there's nothing like that feeling as you pick up speed, actually feel your body accelerate, and you realize that the wind isn't a wind at all, it's just you cutting through the still air like a bullet. There's nothing like that feeling when you know that this is what you do well, and nobody can take it away.

Nobody but L'Austin Space.

He took it away real good—and not so much by beating me, but by purposely making me feel like I wasn't worth a thing. He knew exactly what to say to squash me beneath his big toe. Things like, *"Maybe it's your running shoes that make you slow,"* or *"Maybe next year your legs will grow longer and you'll have a fighting chance,"* or maybe he would just look at me with that silent gloat in his smile after beating me in yet another race.

I don't know why, but it seemed that Coach Shuler always put us in the same races. We would take first and second, but when Austin and I were racing, there were no places, only winner and loser, and I was always, without exception, the loser.

Once I was the best: that one year when Austin's father, who is a professor, took the whole family traipsing around South America for a whole year. It was in seventh grade— first year on the junior high school team—that I finally got to see that finish-line ribbon, to feel it pull across my chest as I crossed the line. I was hot then, the hero, popular— everything I could have wanted.

Then Austin came back, like I knew he would.

I remember the beginning of eighth grade, before the coach knew him. We were lined up for time trials, and just before Austin was to go, he turned to me and gave me that smile. The smile that said, "You're nothing, Jared Mercer . . . and I'll prove it." The coach yelled go, Austin took off, and blew my sixty-yard time sky-high. He beat it by almost half a second, which might not seem like much, but races are lost by hundredths of seconds.

From that moment on I was a backseater again, the Generic Kid, living in the bigger-than-life shadow of L'Austin Space. But this time it was worse, because I had tasted what it was like to be a winner, and Austin was deter- mined to make sure I would never taste it again.

"You take these things too seriously," my father would say. "So, he's faster than you. Big deal. I'll bet there are things you do better than he does."

But there weren't, and my father just didn't understand. It wasn't just that he was faster than me, it was that I was *second,* and nobody on this earth could care less about runners-up.

On that first morning of ninth grade, I watched Austin from the stands. He knew I was there. He had to know; I was the only one in the bleachers. He ran around and around the dirt track in his bright white running shoes that never seemed to get dirty. It looked like he was going to go until the first bell rang, but then he stopped, stepped inside the track, and went to the highest point of the oval. I knew what he was going to do. He did it all the time. His schoolbag sat there at the tip of the oval track. He took his blue digital chronometer—the one the coach gave him after last year's final meet—and set it to zero. Then he took his running shoes and socks off, and stared at an invisible spot in front of him, straight across the middle of the field, to the other tip of the oval. He took his starting position, clicked the chronometer, and took off in his bare feet.

It hurt to watch his speed. He tore through the grass like a racehorse on turf and was at the other end of the oval much too soon.

He looked at the time his chronometer had logged, then he pretended to notice me for the first time. He waved. I waved back. He stretched out his legs, went to get his shoes, then came by the bleachers.

"What's up, Jared?" he said. "Have a good summer?"

"Pretty good. What about you?"

"Great!" he said. He put his foot up on the first bench and stretched his calf muscle. "You like my running shoes?" he asked. "They're Aeropeds. The best running shoe made. Cost almost two hundred bucks."

I nodded.

"Maybe if you had these shoes," said L'Austin, "you *might* be able to come close to giving me some competition this year, huh?"

"Maybe," I said, which wasn't what I wanted to say. I won't tell you what I wanted to say.

"Been workin' out?" he asked.

"Yeah," I said. I had been. Every spare moment I had.

"Good. Me, too. Every day, all summer up at Junior National Running Camp. Hey, guess what?"

"What?"

"I might qualify for the Junior NCAA championships."

"Really."

"Uh-huh. Tough competition, but my time now is averaging a quarter of a second faster than last year's sixty-yard qualifying time, so I've been trying to get it even lower. My dad says if I qualify, then next year he'll find me a private coach and train me for the Olympics." He smiled that I'm-better-than-you smile at me. "So," he said, "what have *you* been up to?"

"Me? Oh, I just went to European Runners Training

Camp, where you run cross-country up and down the Alps all day long with famous Olympic athletes."

"Really?"

I sighed. "No. Actually I just hung around and worked at Burger King making hamburgers. Hard work, that Burger King. Builds muscles in your fingers."

"I'll bet," said Austin.

"You know I was the youngest one they ever had working at that Burger King?"

"Yeah, well that makes sense," said Austin. "I mean, who else are they gonna get to do the stupid flunky work but a kid, right?"

I didn't say anything after that.

"Well, I gotta go change," said L'Austin. "You coming to the first track meeting this afternoon?"

"Of course."

"Well, get there on time," he said, smiling that crocodile smile at me. "They're picking team captain today. I wouldn't want you to miss that." He turned and ran toward the locker room.

Team captain today. Already that smoldering feeling was growing. Austin had done it again. In five minutes he had put me beneath his two-hundred-dollar running shoes, and flattened me like a cigarette butt.

"You ain't got a chance against him," said a voice a few feet away from me. Standing there, right next to the bleachers, was Tyson McGaw, who, when it came to being weird, was head and shoulders above the rest. Tyson had stringy greasy hair, a dirty face, and his left nostril was larger than his right because he spent so much time with his finger in it. Nobody much liked Tyson, and he was definitely not the person I cared to talk to right now. Not after being humiliated by L'Austin Space.

"Why don't you mind your own business, Tyson?" I said. "People don't like you spying on 'em."

"I wasn't spying!" said Tyson, mean and defensively, like he was looking to get into another one of his famous fights. Tyson was an odd bird. Half of the time he seemed kinda nerdy and off in his own greasy little world; the other half of the time he was being nasty and picking fights like he was a tough. The last thing I wanted on the first morning of school was to fight Tyson. Not that I couldn't beat him up; I could—he was kinda weak and scrawny. It's just that he doesn't really fight like a human. He fights more like an animal, kicking and clawing and biting.

"Well, spying or not—whatever you want to call it—don't do it anymore . . . at least not to me, 'cause I don't like it."

I got down from the bleachers, and began to walk toward the school building.

"You really don't stand a chance," mumbled Tyson as I passed him.

"And how would you know?" I yelled into his face. Now I was mad! "You're not on the team—you're not on any team! All you do is watch everybody else's business, and stick your nose in it. Don't you have any business of your own? What goes on between Austin and me has nothing to do with you, got that?"

Tyson shut up. I don't think he expected me to get that mad.

"Just get out of my sight, Tyson. Don't talk to me unless you have something decent to say." I turned and walked toward class. Tyson mumbled something nasty beneath his breath, but I didn't want to push it any further. I ignored him and continued walking.

As I got into the building my anger shifted away from Tyson, and back to Austin. What burned me most was that Tyson was probably right: conceited, arrogant L'Austin Space had all the odds in his favor, and I hated Austin all the more for it. I began to imagine how nice it would be if there was a great conspiracy against all the L'Austin Spaces in the world.

"Now, I want you all to know right up front that this is no namby-pamby team," said Coach Shuler, as he fidgeted with his whistle. "Once you're in, I don't want you all quitting and joining Little League, or a soccer club, or something like that. This might not be high school, and we might not work out five days a week, but anyone who knows me can tell you that I expect hard work. Isn't that right, Jared?"

"Right!" I said, surprised that he called me out of everyone else.

"So if you don't want to be here, leave now."

In the back, two seventh graders, who in one day had already gotten a reputation of being obnoxious, stood and went to the door, laughing. As they left, one of them turned and said, "Adios, Commandant." Some seventh graders laughed. No one who knew Shuler laughed.

Shuler looked at his clipboard. "First of all, boys meet Mondays and Wednesdays; girls meet Tuesdays and Thursdays. Anyone who wants to can practice with both teams . . ."

As Shuler spoke, my mind began to wander. I looked around the gym. It smelled new, but didn't look much different than the old gym. You would think that when a gym burns down, a school would build a nice, new-looking one, but no. This gym was a carbon copy of the old one.

In each corner of the gym, a different team was meeting, and more were meeting outside. It looked like about forty kids were going out for track—a few more boys than girls. By next week that number would be cut in half. The coach never cut anybody, but people just lose interest and drop out.

L'Austin Space sat about ten feet away from me. He sat

in the middle of a crew of seventh graders, already setting himself up to be the "Team Hero" for all of the new kids to look up to.

Shuler flipped a page on his clipboard. "As you can see, we have a beautiful new gym . . . and because of last year's fires, the gym is completely off-limits when a teacher isn't present. The doors will remain locked. That goes for the auditorium, and just about every other unsupervised place. I know you've heard it from all of your teachers—now you're hearing it from me." He flipped another page.

"Next, we have something new this year. Something I think you're going to like. A bunch of the local school districts are getting together to have a sort of mini-Olympics, and yes, there will be track events."

There were various cheers from around the room, including my own.

"That's the good news," said Shuler. "The bad news is that each district enters one team, which means that each school can only have one runner."

Various "Aws" from the group. I kept quiet. I'm sure Austin did, too. I felt a knot begin to form in my stomach.

"Now, before we go down and assign you gym lockers, there's one more order of business."

"The captain!" said Martin Bricker, an eighth grader who had a good chance of being captain next year, but was the only one who thought he would make it this year.

"That's right," said Shuler. "This is for old team members only. Here are pencils and slips of paper. When I say so, I would like all the old team members to come up and fill out a ballot. All you have to do is put the name of the person you would like to be captain this year."

"Don't we get to campaign?" asked L'Austin.

"No, we don't get to campaign," mimicked Shuler. "You all know each other; you don't need any presidential debates. There will be one captain for the boys, and one captain for the girls. Boys vote for boys; girls vote for girls. If you're not sure what you are, ask me and I'll tell you."

Someone lifted Sarah Dozer's hand. She elbowed him in the ribs.

"OK. Come on up. Here's the ballot box, and *please* put the pencils back in the can when you're done."

I filled in Martin Bricker's name, figuring it was low-class to vote for myself, and I certainly wasn't about to vote for Austin.

As Austin approached the ballot box, he turned to me and smiled that crocodile smile that screamed "You loser!" from across the room. I smiled that "We'll see" smile right back at him.

"When will you have the results?" asked Martin.

"They'll be posted on the main bulletin board tomorrow, by lunch."

The group groaned.

"C'mon, it's only one day. Now, when I call your name, come up and I'll give you your locker number."

That night Cheryl and I sat in her old tree house, talking and trying to get my mind off of the election. I never remembered the tree house being so small. I bet it was even too small for Randall to sit in comfortably now. Sometimes I like growing, but at times like that I didn't. I remember when I could lie down across the floor in the tree house. It could fit all three of us—me, Cheryl, and Randall—each in our sleeping bags, late at night, telling ghost stories and drinking chocolate shakes, which were still one of my favorite foods in the world. I loved those days.

Now I couldn't even sit in it without bending my knees. It had been almost a year since I had been in it. Cheryl only lived down the street, but we never had much of a reason to go up into the tree house anymore.

It was Cheryl who had said, "Let's talk in the tree house," and I had said, "Fine," figuring it would cheer me up. Now, an hour later, the twilight was more twi than light, and the early September chill had come rolling in off the ocean.

"What else?" said Cheryl. "Keep thinking."

"I don't know, I can't think of any more."

"Don't you have any imagination?"

"No."

"Yes, you do," she said.

"OK . . . umm." I thought hard. "I know . . . I would hang him by his toes . . . upside down . . . over a bear trap."

Cheryl laughed. "Now you're getting really gross."

"You asked for it. Your turn."

"OK. Next time she sings . . . I would throw roses at her, like that guy did, for her to put behind her ears. Only I would make sure they had lots of thorns on 'em!"

I grimaced.

"Your turn," she said.

"I would set Austin loose in Lion Country Wild Animal Park, and see how fast he runs. Next."

"Oohh! Vicious! Let's see . . . I would . . . I would fill her little lunch-box thermos with hydrochloric acid."

"Not fair," I said. "I said that one at the wedding."

"Well, then how about a king cobra in her lunch box?"

"No, wait . . . I've got one for you," I said. "Why don't we get her a nice date . . . with Tyson McGaw?"

"Ugh! A fate worse than death!" We both laughed good and hard just trying to imagine Rebecca and slimy Tyson McGaw together. What a match!

"I can't believe we're really this nasty!" I said.

"But isn't it fun?" said Cheryl.

I guess it was. It was sort of like watching those horror movies. Sure, they're sick and gross and bloody and all that, but everyone still loves them, right?

"I mean, it's not like we're really doing anything to them," said Cheryl. "We're not *really* mean and terrible, it's just a game. Everybody has someone that really irks them, and there's nothing wrong with pretending, right?"

"Wait a second, I just had a brainstorm," I said. "We'll pay some bozo to pretend to teach Austin to walk on hot coals, and when he finally goes for it, he'll burn off his feet. So much for running!"

"You're awful," laughed Cheryl. Then she stopped laughing, and thought for a moment. Without the sound of our voices, the night seemed very quiet. I don't think I heard as much as one cricket.

"Hey," she said, "wouldn't it be weird if any of those things actually happened to Austin or Rebecca? Like somebody up there was listening?"

"I'll make sure I keep my eye out for bear traps," I said. She laughed. I could barely see her now, in the shadows on the other side of the tree house. Like I said, it was small; I could feel her Reeboks touching my Nikes. I wiggled my feet, and she wiggled back, like we were playing footsy, or something dumb like that. I looked over the edge railing. It was clear that night. No fog like the last few nights. Cheryl's house was the last on the street, and from there you could just barely see the ocean between the trees, a quarter mile away. It was my favorite time of day—when the faint blue glow against the horizon is just enough to make everything look black against it, just after the colors have faded from the sky.

Back when we were kids, I always loved talking with

Cheryl, and even with Randall, in the tree house at this time of day. Ghost stories, or even just stupid-talk. Now that we were older and busier, it seemed as though I never really got to talk to Cheryl alone when it was quiet like this. It was different from the old days, but I still liked it. I wiggled my feet again, and she wiggled back.

"Maybe we shouldn't have done all that before," she said.

"What?"

"Talk mean about Rebecca and Austin. It's like I feel guilty now."

Now that we had stopped, I began to feel it, too. "Well, it was your idea."

"Thanks, now I feel worse."

"Sorry," I said. Then I gave her her own speech back. "It's only words," I said. "It's only like . . . sticking your tongue out at them. That's all. Like you said, it's only pretend. We're not hurting anybody."

"Right."

"It gets out all our frustrations and stuff, so we don't go around being angry at them all day."

"Right."

Somehow I still don't think I convinced her. I didn't convince myself, either. I couldn't—not when my mind was still filled with all those nasty, ridiculous things that could be brought down upon L'Austin Space. What bothered me most was that, like Cheryl said, it was fun. I didn't like feeling that it was fun.

I moved closer to Cheryl. Somehow I felt that moving closer to her would make that creepy feeling go away.

"Do you really hate Austin?" Cheryl asked. I couldn't see her talking now, it was too dark. I could just barely make out her shape against the trees behind her.

"I don't know," I said. "Do you really hate Rebecca?"

Cheryl sighed and didn't answer for a long time. Then she said, "It's not really hate. She's my cousin. I care about her . . . but sometimes I think she enjoys making me feel lousy."

"I know Austin does."

"Do you really hate Austin, Jared?" she asked again.

"I don't know," I said for a second time. I really didn't know. "It's all gotten so confused."

She thought for a good long time. "Would you be happy if Austin Pace moved far away?" she asked very matter-of-factly.

"Yes," I said.

"Would you be happy if he got hurt so bad that he couldn't run fast?"

"I don't think so. I think I'd feel sorry for him."

"How about if he died?"

"Cheryl! C'mon!"

"Sorry, dumb question." She was silent for a long, long

time. She was thinking about something. I could tell. Then she finally spoke, very quietly, and slowly.

"I know what the real question is," she said. "The real question to find out whether or not you hate him."

"What?"

"The question is . . . if there were a way for you to make it happen . . . would you wish that Austin Pace had never been born?"

The cold of the night hit me just then, but I don't think it was just the cold. It was something more. Something inside, not out. And it was because I knew the answer to that question, and I didn't like that answer at all.

"Would you?" she asked again.

"Yes," I whispered.

And then she whispered back, "I know how that feels."

The breeze played with the dying leaves above us. The chill got stronger. Before, I had just felt nasty. Now I felt weird. Weird and uncomfortable—with myself, and with that question. Do I wish L'Austin Space had never been born? Yes. Yes, I wished that. As much as I hated myself for wishing that, deep down, really deep down, I did feel that way, and I couldn't change that. It was scary.

"Cheryl . . . I'm spooked out."

"Me, too," she said.

"It's getting cold . . ." I said.

"Maybe we should go in."

Cheryl went first, and I followed her down.

"You really do feel that way, too, huh?"

"I don't want to talk about that anymore. Let's talk about something nice."

But we didn't talk about anything nice. We didn't talk much about anything at all. That good feeling we had when we first climbed into the tree house was gone, and wouldn't come back for the rest of the night. We went in, watched ten minutes of TV with her brother, then I hopped on my bike and rode home. I tried to chase that eerie feeling away by burying my head in that first night's homework.

It worked. By morning the feeling was gone. I felt like my old self and went on as if what we had discovered about ourselves in the tree house that night meant absolutely nothing at all.

Ignoring that night was a mistake—not the first one, and not the last one either. Maybe that feeling was meant to be a warning, a bright red alarm flashing in our eyes. If it was, we were both too stupid to notice it.

The Fire
and
the Agony

PEOPLE WERE MILLING around the phys-ed bulletin board before classes. Ours wasn't the only team choosing captains that day, and everyone there waited impatiently for each coach to put up the results.

I wasn't one of the kids waiting. Sure, I wanted to be captain, but I didn't want to think about it. The more I thought about it, the more worried I would get, and I'd feel miserable until the results went up. Better to think about anything else until then. I thought about my new teachers, my old friends, what I would have for lunch, anything but the track team and Austin Pace in his million-dollar Aeropeds that never got dirty and looked like they came from planet Krypton, or someplace like that.

I wandered around a bit before the homeroom bell rang, looking for people I hadn't seen the day before. People really do change in one summer. Charlie Garcias had grown like six inches since June, certain locations on Abbie Singer had begun to inflate, if you know what I mean, and half of everyone I knew seemed to have gotten rid of their braces. I talked to Ralphy Sherman, who said that he made a movie in Hollywood over the summer. Ralphy was always good for a laugh, because he had never uttered a word of truth in his entire life.

Pretty soon I forgot all about the track team, and was in a good mood—such a good mood that I even said hello to Tyson McGaw. He grunted back, then five minutes later got himself into a fight with some kid whose name I don't remember.

Watching Tyson get into fights was a school tradition. Personally, I never got into a real fight with him. Like I said before, Tyson fought like an animal, and I wanted nothing to do with that. Just looking at him you could tell that something wasn't quite right; his eyes were kind of far away, like he wasn't seeing you, and his stringy, matted hair was just plain ugly—it seemed no amount of combing could help that. Tyson was definitely not a mother's dream.

Mr. Greene saw the fight and ran down the hall. Mr. Greene was a vice principal, but doubled as the school guidance counselor, which must have been a tough job, since so many kids go wacko during junior high.

After Mr. Greene had broken up the fight (which wasn't much of a fight; it was more like Tyson doing an impersonation of the Tasmanian devil), everyone in the hall began to applaud and laugh at Tyson as he continued struggling with

Greene. I have to admit, I laughed a little, too—like I said, it was a school tradition.

Mr. Greene held him as he struggled, then Tyson turned to Greene and screamed out a whole lot of words I don't want to repeat, and started breathing like a bull ready to charge.

"You know what he did?" he screamed at Greene.

"What did he do, Tyson?"

"He called me a slimeball!"

I laughed right away—I just couldn't help it. It was the way he said it, with all that anger in his voice, long and drawn out: "sliyyyyyym-ballll."

Everyone laughed, but I guess I must have laughed the loudest, because Tyson broke away from Greene and stomped up to me.

"You think that's funny, huh?" he yelled, almost ready to pull back his fist and hit me.

"You touch me, Tyson, and I swear I'll flatten you!" I said. "I'll . . . I'll hang you by your toenails over a bear trap!"

That one really sent him for a loop. He looked at me with those weird eyes, trying to figure out how that would feel. For a split second, I felt bad for him. Here he was, this nutty kid in a frenzy, and everyone was laughing at him. He must have felt terrible. I almost felt like saying, *"It's OK, Tyson, you're not a slimeball, take it easy,"* just to make him feel better, but then everyone around me began to laugh even harder, and Tyson stormed off.

Greene gave me this dirty look that said, *"Bear trap? I'll give you bear trap! Bang! Zoom!"* and ran after Tyson. Yes, school was the same as ever.

As the homeroom bell rang, I heard a voice behind me.

"Jared, I'd like to speak with you for a minute."

I recognized the voice right away. I turned to see Coach Shuler. You know that feeling you get when you think something great is gonna happen, and your heart misses a beat, and you get shivers down your spine? Well, that's what I felt just then. Why would Coach Shuler pull me aside to talk to me unless he had good news for me about the captaincy?

"Hi, Coach, what's up?" I said cheerfully.

"Got a minute?"

"Yeah."

"Great. Why don't you come into my office."

I followed him down the hall, and into the gym, where it was much quieter. Our footsteps echoed in the huge empty gym as we crossed it. It was cold and the air had the sour smell of the floor varnish. We went into the gym office.

"Have a seat," he said, then he picked up his clipboard and began to look at it. He sat in the other chair, behind the desk. "I totaled up the results," he said.

"Yeah?" I said, trying to sound like I didn't really care.

"It was pretty close."

"Yeah?"

He looked up from his clipboard. I really couldn't read his expression. He had a poker face, I guess; you could never

tell what was in his head. He stalled, keeping me in sus-
pense. I didn't have a poker face; I knew all the expectation
was in my eyes. In my lap I had my fingers crossed so hard
that my knuckles were turning white.

"You didn't get it, Jared. I'm sorry."

At first it was like I didn't quite hear him. My fingers
were still crossed, as if crossing them could change what he
had said. I still held my breath, but then what my ears had
heard made its way into my brain.

You know that sinking feeling—the kind you get about
ten seconds before you realize that you're going to throw up?
Well, I didn't feel like I was going to throw up, but that sinking feeling stayed around for a long time.

Before I went into his office, I had been prepared to lose,
but then he called me in, and I was sure that I had won.
Why couldn't he have just let me find out when he posted it?
I could have handled that. It wouldn't have been so bad; I
would have just looked and walked away. But now he had
gotten my hopes up, and I couldn't just walk away; I had to
sit there and feel lousy.

"Like I said," continued the coach, "it was a close race.
You and Austin were neck and neck all the way." He began
to fiddle with his clipboard. If it wasn't his clipboard, it was
his whistle, if it wasn't his whistle it was his glasses—he always fiddled with something. "Listen, I know how much you
wanted to be captain, and because of all your hard work, I'm

going to make you a very special offer. As runner-up, you are entitled to something very special, so I'm making you assistant coach."

"Assistant coach?" I said. It might not sound so bad to you, but you have to understand that assistant coach was a position usually given to some younger kid who was not a good enough runner to be on the team. He might as well have told me I was team mascot. Assistant coach!

"That's right."

"Well, what do I get to do?"

"Take attendance, get equipment, stuff like that."

Well, what was I supposed to say to that? Austin gets all the glory and power of being team captain, and I get to take attendance. I tried to be enthusiastic, but I just couldn't, and the coach could see it in my eyes. I didn't have a poker face.

"Thanks," I said.

"You don't seem too happy about it."

"No, I'm happy. I'm just a little upset about not being captain. That's all."

"Sure, I understand. You can hang around here for a few minutes if you like. I'll give you a late pass for homeroom."

"Naah, that's OK." I'm sure he could tell by my voice that it wasn't OK. I didn't have a poker voice either.

"Listen," he said, "there's always high school."

"Right," I said, silently thinking how L'Austin Space would win again when we were seniors in high school. "Thanks," I said.

"Least I could do. You're a good kid, Jared. I feel bad for you."

"Naah, don't feel bad for me. I don't want you feeling bad for me."

"Well, I mean that I think sometimes life gives people the short end of the stick, you know, and I think you deserve more."

"Thanks," I said, for the twelve-hundredth time.

"See you this afternoon?"

"Yep."

"Be early," he said, "so you can take attendance."

The hall was empty when I left the gym, except for one kid; none other than L'Austin Space himself was standing outside the gym doors. He was waiting for me. It wasn't a coincidence.

"Oh, you spoke to the coach already, huh?" he said.

"Yep."

"So he told you I won?"

"How did you already know?"

"He spoke to me first," said Austin. "You don't think he'd tell you before he told me, do you?" Austin waited for an answer, but I didn't give him one.

"I bet you'll like being team secretary," he said.

"Assistant coach!"

"All it really is is team secretary. Hey, I'll make sure to give you lots of memos to type. Maybe you can come over to my house sometime and answer some phones," he said, laughing.

I turned and walked down the hall. He followed, his Aeropeds gliding across the floor. I wanted to step on them, and leave nice gray tread marks on the snow-white leather toes.

"It's not secretary," I said.

"All right, 'gopher' then."

I stopped. "What?"

"You know, Gopher: 'hey Jared, go-pher this, hey Jared, go-pher that, hey Jared, go-pher, go-pher, go-pher.' "

I just scowled at him. He saw the anger in my unpoker face, and laughed. "Just kidding," he said, in the nastiest, most obnoxious tone a person could come up with, then he laughed harder and turned away, his Aeropeds bouncing off down the hallway, squeaking on the floor.

I felt more humiliated than I'd felt in a long time as I walked down the hall. It wasn't the fact that I was assistant coach that bothered me, it was the fact that Austin knew first, and as usual, made fun of me, calling me "Gopher." It was bad enough to feel hidden in his shadow, but to be humiliated; that was something else. He was twisting the knife.

How would I feel if Austin Pace had never been born? Let's not talk about it.

The alarm went off at 1:30. That's right, you guessed it: another school fire. I can't say I wasn't glad to hear the alarm bell; I hadn't been able to concentrate all day because of what had happened that morning. At least now I could feel angry without having to pay attention to teachers at the same time.

Used to be nobody raised much of a fuss when the fire alarm went off. The teachers would just get the class up and funnel them "in an orderly manner" down the stairway and out into the field. Now it was much quicker, and much more serious. Used to be they were all drills or false alarms, but last year there were three real fires. The last one burned down the gym.

Now, as we marched into the hall, I could swear I already smelled smoke.

The scene out in the field was much more chaotic than any of the teachers could stand for. Kids were running in the field, and the neat little rows of classes were breaking down into mobs of kids—a good many of them pressing up against the fence to see the smoke pouring out of the cafeteria. It wasn't a whole lot of smoke, but it was enough to cause a commotion.

I didn't really care to watch the fire; I had my own problems to think about. If I sound heartless, it isn't because I didn't care about anyone left in the school. I had overheard the principal say that the school had been cleared, and there was nothing to worry about, except for the cafeteria burning down (which, believe me, is exactly what the cafeteria deserved).

While the cafeteria smoked, I fumed, still filled with the anger Austin had put in me that morning.

"I don't want to talk about it!" I told Cheryl when she asked me about the track team. She knew exactly what I meant when I said, "And don't ask again."

"Well, join the club," she said.

"Why, what's wrong with you?"

"Oh, nothing," she said. "It's just that the play they're doing this year is *Annie*."

"So?"

"So, guess what snotty little brat is absolutely perfect for the role?"

"Rebecca's trying out?"

"I don't even think she has to. They'll just look at her and give her the role."

Cheryl continued to complain at me about Rebecca and other things. I turned to look at the school. The firefighters were standing by the fire truck, doing nothing in particular, which meant that the fire was not a big one and had been put out right away. The cafeteria had been saved, although it would probably smell like smoke for the rest of the year.

We all knew there would be no more school that day; not till they were positive there was no fire left, and the building had a chance to air out. Still, they couldn't let us go home until 3:00, and so the school yard began to resemble a junior high school riot, with kids playing all sorts of unruly games that made the teachers all start pulling out their hair.

". . . a club," said Cheryl.

"Huh?" I asked, not having heard her.

"I said we should form a club of all the kids who are second-best."

I laughed. "Yeah, right . . . and one by one do away with everyone in our way! *Mwaaah-ha-haa!*"

"No, I'm serious. We could have a club just for fun— something that only we could have, and none of the 'unbeatable' kids could be in it, a second-best club!"

"That's a stupid idea," I said.

"No it's not! We could all go and do things, and have fun, and really make the 'unbeatable' kids jealous that we thought of it before they did. We'll be one up on them for a change."

"Yeah? Who would be in this club?"

"I don't know. We'd have to think about it for a while, and come up with some names. I'll bet there are lots of kids who'd want to be in it—my brother, for instance."

"Nobody else'll want to do it. They'll laugh at us."

"But if they don't, Jared, we could be starting something big, a secret club that will go on for years after we've gone on to high school!"

I thought about this. Cheryl always had a way of convincing me of things. But this time she wasn't the one who convinced me. It was someone else.

"Hey, Jared," someone called. It was that familiar voice, a voice I didn't want to hear. I could almost see those Aeropeds and that red hair, and those long bony arms.

"Hey, Jared, wanna race?" asked Austin. "First race of the season."

So this was it. The challenge. Austin was always the one to challenge first. Usually he waited until the second week, when he had seen me run and was absolutely sure he'd be able to beat me. This time he asked on the second day, and there were too many kids around for me to turn down the challenge.

"Don't you think it'd be better if we waited till the field was clear?" I said.

"Isn't this clear enough?"

I turned around. Sure enough, the field was clear enough to race. Austin had come over with about ten kids, and more kids were joining us, because everyone knew what he was up to, and everyone knew about our rivalry.

"Maybe we should wait until your legs grow some more,"

he said. Everyone laughed. I laughed, too; better to be laughed *with* than laughed *at*, right? Inside I wasn't laughing, though.

"Fine, then," I said. "Right now."

Austin smiled that crocodile smile. "Greg, go about sixty yards, and judge us." Greg Miller, one of the new seventh graders on the team, obeyed, as if he had been given an order by God.

So this is where it begins, I thought, this year's competition. This year's war. I felt strong, I felt ready to run, I felt like I always felt when I raced with Austin—that maybe this time I would beat him.

We got down into starting position, then Austin got up.

"Wait," he said, and took off his precious shoes, then his socks. He was going to run barefoot. "OK." He got back down. "Ready to lose?" he asked.

I didn't answer.

Martin Bricker got ready to start us, as more and more kids turned to watch. Even teachers were watching. So this is where it begins.

"On your mark . . . get set . . . *go!*"

I took off like a bullet, cutting through the wind and pounding the grass with every last bit of my strength. I didn't turn to look, but I could see in the corner of my eye that we were neck and neck.

Ten yards were gone.

I looked toward Greg, down the field, and concentrated on turning everything I had into power.

This is for every time you beat me in races as a kid!

I pushed harder.

And this is for when you came back to do it again last year!

I pushed harder.

And this is for how you made me feel this morning!

I pushed harder.

We were still neck and neck.

Thirty yards were gone. Thirty to go.

The cheers faded away behind us.

And this is for challenging me in front of the whole school, and this is for everything you'll ever try to do to me for the rest of our lives, and this is for those stupid running shoes you wear!

Forty yards gone.

I was ahead of him by a foot! I was beating him! I pushed harder.

Fifteen yards to go! Fifteen to go!

And then, like he'd been holding it all back, he flew out in front of me. He didn't inch out, he flew out, like I was standing still. He moved like a machine in fast forward; a ship blasting into hyperspace. He was a foot in front of me. Two feet. Three feet. He turned to look at me, and smiled that awful smile of his.

I lunged. I dove forward in a wild attempt to reach the finish line before he did, but he was there before I hit the ground. I was moving so fast that I skidded along the grass, skinning my elbows and ruining my pants.

The Agony of Defeat.

I felt like that skier who wipes out on the ski jump every Sunday on *Wide World of Sports*. The Agony of Defeat: skinned elbows and ruined pants and a laughing L'Austin Space.

By now kids were crowding around Austin.

"Wow, did you see Austin take off?"

"Wow, he really beat him bad!"

"Wow, Austin's so fast!"

Wow this, and wow that. Austin was loving every last bit of it. They crowded around him and left me there on the ground to examine my elbows.

"You shouldn't race Austin, kid," said a seventh grader. "Austin beats everybody."

Austin looked down at me. He was barely winded. "You ran pretty good . . . for a gopher!" he said, and everyone laughed.

"Gopher!" they all said. "Gopher, Gopher, Gopher!" Austin raised his hands to conduct them as they all chanted in unison: "Go-PHER! Go-PHER! Go-PHER!" over and over again.

I could have killed him! I could have ripped him limb from limb, but then I thought about Tyson McGaw. No. I wasn't Tyson. I was civilized, and I wasn't going to attack

Austin. Instead I stood up, brushed myself off, and waited till the gopher-chanting stopped. Then I looked Austin straight in the face, and put out my hand.

"Nice race, Austin." I shook his hand. Let me tell you, it took all my strength to do it, too.

"Yeah," he said. "See ya around, Gopher."

I turned and left while everyone crowded around Austin. My elbows had just begun hurting.

Cheryl was there waiting for me. That's one thing about her; she was always there, and she never laughed at me either.

"Are you OK?" she asked.

I looked back toward Austin, then turned to Cheryl and asked, "So, what are we going to call our club?"

The Charter
at
Stonehenge

I DON'T THINK anyone knew what used to be there, but whatever it had been, only the old stone foundation remained, in a clearing in the woods. The stones were worn and covered with moss. Inside the rectangular stone foundation was a pit about six feet deep and twenty feet across, filled with bushes and trees. It could have been there for a hundred years—nobody knew.

Cheryl, Randall, and I had found it years ago, exploring as kids, but it seemed too eerie to play in, so we had left it alone, filing it away in our heads for future reference. The old foundation sat there in the thick woods between Cheryl's house and the ocean, waiting. I had always thought of the foundation as waiting—waiting for someone to use it again, I guess, or maybe just waiting to disappear into the earth, like the building that once stood above it had.

It was waiting, all right, and on the second Friday of ninth grade, I had this certain exciting feeling that it was waiting for us.

As Cheryl and I stood on the outer edge of the deep stone foundation, looking into the pit, Cheryl said, "This is great! I couldn't think of a better place to have our meetings!"

I walked around the edge until I came to a place where the foundation had given way, and the earth sloped down into the pit. I climbed down into the center, and Cheryl followed.

"It looks like it could almost be magical," she said.

"Maybe it's haunted or something."

"Well, don't go and make it all spooky," she said. But it was spooky already; spooky in a fun sort of way, like the mummy cases in the museum, or a ghost town. There was a feeling to the place that made anything we could possibly do there seem very, very important. It would give our club meetings a hint of mystery.

"What time is it?" I asked.

"Four-fifteen. They'll be here in fifteen minutes."

As I looked around, I began to see things you couldn't see from up on the ledge. There were old green Coke bottles, and aluminum cans with the old-fashioned pull-off tabs that they stopped making years ago. There were designs on the cans that I didn't even recognize. For all I knew they could have been here since the building came down. All around us were little bits of the past that no one had touched for years and years. It was magical—like that Stonehenge place in England, mysterious rocks with a hidden history.

"Let's call this place Stonehenge," I said to Cheryl.

"Great!" she said. "I like that." She climbed back up to the edge and sat on a moss-covered cinder block at the lip of the pit. The edge of Stonehenge.

"I feel like . . . a witch," she said.

"You look like one!" I said. She had stepped right into that one!

"Shut up! You know what I mean. It's like we could conjure up ghosts here!"

"What time is it?" I asked.

"Four-twenty," said Cheryl.

At first, I had felt funny talking to kids about this club; I was afraid they would laugh in my face—but no one did. Picking out the kids for the club became like a game. Cheryl and I would keep our eyes open, watching for kids in our exact situation; kids who were second-best, were miserable about it, and had to live under the shadow of some nasty "unbeatable" person, who rubbed their noses in it every day.

We ruled out some kids right away, others took longer, but finally we came up with a list of five kids who would be perfect. We didn't want a big group; seven, including us, was just fine. One by one, either Cheryl or I spoke to them when no one else was around. And you know what? Every single one of them wanted to be in the club—The Shadow Club—as Cheryl and I named it. So we called the first meeting, then marked the trees so that everyone could find our secret meeting place in the woods. At any second they would converge on the old foundation, and the Shadow Club would be born.

"What time is it?" I asked.

Cheryl looked at me with those give-me-a-break sort of eyes, and said, "Stop being ridiculous," so I didn't ask anymore.

I climbed back down into Stonehenge to start up the campfire.

The sun was near the horizon and shadows were getting long and dark when everyone finally arrived. By now the little campfire I had started in the center of the big square foundation pit was burning strong. It wasn't dark, and it wasn't cold, and we didn't have marshmallows to roast, so the campfire didn't seem to make much sense, but it was there for a very good reason that only Cheryl and I knew.

"I guess we should start by formally introducing ourselves," I said.

"But why?" asked Randall. "We all know each other already."

"Shut up," said Cheryl. "You'll see."

"I'll start," I said, clearing my throat. I had practiced my speech a few times at home, so I didn't feel funny being the first one to go. "My name is Jared Mercer. I am the second-best runner in the school, second to Austin Pace, the most conceited, obnoxious . . . Is anyone here friends with Austin?"

Nobody raised their hand, so I continued.

". . . conceited, obnoxious, pain-in-the-neck kid ever to be on any track team. He takes every chance he gets to make me feel lousy, just because I'm not as fast as he is." I paused for effect. "I hate Austin Pace." I turned to Cheryl, and she began.

"My name is Cheryl Gannett. I am, and have always been, the second-best singer, dancer, and all-around performer in my family. Even my own mother forgets I can sing. Now it's the same way in school. My cousin Rebecca, who thinks she's God's gift to the universe, gets all the attention. I hate Rebecca."

"I get it!" said Randall. "OK, it's my turn. My name is Randall Gannett, and I'm the best swimmer in the eighth grade."

"Randall . . . ," Cheryl said impatiently.

"Shh!" said Randall. "Like I said, I'm the best swimmer, but Drew Landers thinks he's better than me . . . but he's not."

"Randall, you can't do that," said Cheryl.

"Why not? It's true!"

"You have to admit it," I said. "You have to admit to being second-best, otherwise you can't be in the club."

"But he's not better than me!"

"No?" said Cheryl. "Did you ever beat him in a race?"

Randall looked like a cornered animal. "Almost . . . ," he said.

"So he *is* faster."

"He cheats!" said Randall.

"How can you cheat in swimming?"

"Well, he's taller! If he wasn't taller, I would win." Randall shut up after that one, and looked around the circle, feeling embarrassed.

"Maybe we should go on, and come back to you later," suggested Cheryl.

"No, I'll go," said Randall, defeated. Now he looked down and fidgeted with a stick. "I'm the second-best swimmer, OK? Drew Landers is better than me; he always beats me by a tenth of a second, and then he laughs at me. He even laughs at me during swim meets, when everyone on the team is supposed to be cheering one another on." Randall looked up for a moment, then back down at his twig. A sad, but mean expression came over his face. "Even though I take second place all the time, he still laughs at me. And he calls me Duckfeet, because my feet are a little big. And next year when all the ninth graders graduate, he'll be the best on the team, probably the captain, and he'll still laugh at me every day. I hate Drew Landers." Randall looked up at Cheryl. "Are you happy?"

"That'll do," said Cheryl.

Jason cleared his throat to get everyone's attention. He was rarin' to go. "My name is Jason Perez." He took off his glasses, probably feeling self-conscious about them. He was also self-conscious about being fat, even though he wasn't fat anymore; he had grown into his weight. "I play trumpet," said Jason. "I've been playing for four years, and I'm finally getting good enough to play first trumpet for band, and I've been taking extra lessons, but then last year, David Berger just up and decides he wants to learn trumpet, and in like three months, he's better than everyone, so he gets every single solo, and every single award, and I get absolutely nothing, ever, no matter how hard I practice, and I really hate David Berger!" He stopped for a second, and we all thought he was done, but then he started up again. "Last June, when they picked kids for the Young Musicians Society, did I get picked? No! David Berger, David Berger, all anybody ever hears about is David Berger! I can't stand him, and now he's been picked to play for the high school band—can you believe it? And then . . ."

"Jason," I said, interrupting, "how do you say all that without breathing?" There were a few giggles from around the circle.

"Well, sorry," said Jason. "I thought you wanted to know."

"You can tell us after everybody's had a chance," said Cheryl.

Everyone turned to Abbie, who had her strawberry blonde hair in some new style that was hard not to stare at.

"Well, as you know, I'm Abbie Singer, and I have absolutely no idea why I'm here." And that's all she said at first.

"C'mon, Abbie, you know why," said Cheryl.

"No, I really don't. I'm not second-best at anything—I don't even think I'm third-best. I do hate Vera Donaldson, like you said when you first told me about this club thing, Cheryl, but she is definitely not better than me in anything."

I turned to Cheryl, but Cheryl didn't say anything. It was Jason who spoke, very softly. "I know why you're here," he said, looking down at the pair of glasses he held in his hands. "You're here because you're the second-prettiest girl in school."

Abbie thought about this. "Is that why, Cheryl?"

"Well, you *are* the second most popular girl in school."

Abbie smiled. "Yeah, I guess I am, aren't I?"

"Vera Donaldson is a snot," said Jason. I thought that was too nice a word for her.

"Well, not everyone thinks so. She's the most popular girl in school," said Abbie, "and she hates my guts. I don't know why, but every time there's a guy who likes me, she always steals him away first, just for fun, or tells him nasty things about me. Do you know how it feels for people to say nasty stuff about you like that? And none of it's true! Absolutely none of it!" She clenched her teeth and her hands rolled into fists. "Just thinking about her makes my head hurt."

"Say it!" said Cheryl.

"I hate Vera Donaldson!"

O.P., who was next, looked around a bit nervously. She had been quiet all this time and knew perfectly well why she was here. O.P. was Korean, I think, but she didn't have any accent at all.

"I'm Karin Han . . . and . . . I guess I'm smart. I have the second-highest math and reading scores in the ninth grade. I get the second-best grades in just about everything, and Tommy Nickols always gets the best."

"Ughh! He's such a bozo," said Abbie.

"If I get a ninety-eight on a test," she continued, "then Tommy will get a ninety-nine. All the time. So last year he started to call me O.P., and now everyone does. It stands for 'One Point.' "

Randall giggled and Cheryl elbowed him.

"Yeah, everyone thinks it's funny. I don't mind being called it, but I hate it when Tommy Nickols says it. I guess I hate Tommy Nickols."

Last in the circle was Darren Collins, whose legs seemed longer than just about everyone's whole body. He was fourteen, but was getting pretty close to six feet already. I'll give you one guess what he did.

"Yeah, I'm second-best, too," admitted Darren. "I've

never gotten MVP on any basketball team, I was always next in line—someone else always beat me out. Usually it doesn't really bug me that much, but for two years Eric Kilfoil has been making me look like a fool on the court all the time. He's like turned me into the team mascot or something, and makes everybody think I'm a dumb jock—but I'm not, I get good grades. Then he does these Harlem Globetrotter things to me, you know, like bouncing the ball off the top of my head, and then getting the shot in—and everyone laughs. Once, I got so mad, I stepped on his face and got taken out of the game. I hate Eric Kilfoil."

And it was back to me. By now the shadows were getting even longer; it was almost time for the sky to turn colors. A soft wind blew down into Stonehenge and the campfire crackled. The first part was done. Now came part two.

"Cheryl?" I asked.

"Oh, I forgot." Cheryl opened her folder and pulled out the charter of the club, written on imitation parchment paper. "Everyone has to sign this," she said, then began to recite the charter:

THE SHADOW CLUB CHARTER

We, the undersigned, do hereby form the Shadow Club—an organization dedicated to the righteous indignation of its members toward all those obnoxious

*unbeatable people who make our lives miserable
every single day. We shall no longer suffer their
slings and arrows. We will be proud of who we are,
and not let them get the better of us.*

*We hereafter swear loyalty and secrecy to the
Shadow Club, and all of its members, for as long as
this charter shall exist.*

I had to smile. Cheryl's mom was a lawyer, and only the
daughter of a lawyer could come up with such a legal-
sounding charter.

"What's righteous indignation?" asked Jason.

"It means we have a good reason to be p.o.'d," said O.P.

Cheryl and I had already signed it, so she passed it on to
Randall and gave him a pen.

"Shouldn't we sign this in blood?" asked Randall.

"No way!" said Abbie from across the fire. "I refuse to
bleed."

"Well, it was just an idea. I figured it would make it more
official."

Randall signed it, and passed it to Jason. The charter
went around the fire, came back to Cheryl, and she put it
back into her folder.

"Is that it?" asked Darren.

"One more thing," I said. "The pictures."

"Oh, right," said Darren.

Everyone reached into one pocket or another. I couldn't believe it; everyone had managed to get a picture.

"I hope you know how much trouble I went through to get this," said Randall. "I had to search through Drew Landers' swim locker. I found it in his wallet."

"I had to go and take a picture of David Berger," said Jason. "He had no idea why I did it."

"Good," I said. "Don't tell anyone why. Remember, no one tells anyone about anything we do in the club. That's part of the rules."

"Why do we need the pictures?" asked O.P.

"Symbolic gesture," said Cheryl.

Everyone held a picture of their mortal enemy in their hands. I held a picture of Austin. It had been a picture of both of us together, but I cut it in half. He smiled up at me from the picture and the smile said, *You'll never beat me!*

"We'll see," I muttered to the photo, then made sure everyone was watching, and tossed the picture into the fire. The edges flared, the colors faded, Austin's red hair turned brown, then black, and those eyes died, shriveling to ashes. We'll see, I thought.

Cheryl went next, and everyone followed, until the last picture had been thrown into the fire.

"I now pronounce that the Shadow Club has begun!"

The wind became a bit stronger, and the fire crackled. Everyone sat around the fire there in Stonehenge, watching the ashes of the pictures disappear. Then, they all slowly looked up, then at each other, then at Cheryl and me.

"So?" said Darren.

"So, what?" I asked.

"So, what do we do now?"

Suddenly my feeling of power flew away. I hadn't thought about that. I hadn't thought past the burning of the pictures at all. What came next? I didn't know.

"So what's this club going to do?" asked Abbie. I looked at Cheryl, who I figured would have all the answers, but she just looked back at me the same way I looked at her.

"Well, we go and do stuff," I said.

"Like what?" asked Jason.

"I don't know . . . go to the movies . . ."

"Go bowling," suggested Cheryl.

"Play games," I said.

"I got a miniature chess set with me," said O.P. "Anyone wanna play?"

"Give me a break," said Darren.

"I guess we could just hang out together," said Randall.

"Boooring!" said Darren.

"He's right," said Abbie. "It does sound boring."

"What about miniature golf?" suggested Cheryl.

"Boooooooring!" said Jason and Darren together.

"Well, we could sell stuff and raise money," said Cheryl.

"For what?"

"For . . . Shadow Club T-shirts?" said Cheryl.

"Booooooooooooring!" they all said.

"Hey, I like you guys and everything," said Abbie, standing up, "but if I want to go out and do stuff like that, I have my own friends."

"Me, too," said Jason.

Darren stood up. "You know something, Jared?" Darren waited until everyone else was listening. "I think this was a really dumb idea."

"No it's not!" I said, standing up as well. I was a head shorter than him, and at that moment felt even smaller. Everyone seemed ready to agree that the club was stupid. Everything had been going so well; why did all this have to happen now?

"What's so good about it?" asked Darren. "So, you got us here, and we burned some pictures, and we signed a piece of paper. Big deal. I got better things to do on Friday afternoon. Why should I come to these dumb meetings?"

"Because . . ." I said, "because . . . we have stuff to do!"

"Like what?" asked Randall. Even Randall was a traitor! For a second I felt like it was over. Cheryl and I had lost complete control. But then I closed my eyes, thought for a second, waited until I felt the calm come back to my voice, and when it did, I had an idea—a fantastic idea that might just save the club!

"Like what?" asked Randall again.

"We have secret things we're going to do."

"Like what?" demanded Randall, getting annoyed.

I smiled. "Just like the charter says, we're dedicated to fight the unbeatables, and that's just what we'll do. We'll wage a secret war against them . . . a war . . . of practical jokes, to embarrass and humiliate them, just like they do to us!"

It took a few seconds to sink in. Jason smiled first, then O.P., then Randall.

"Oh, I love it!" said Abbie.

"Intense!" said O.P.

"Classic!" said Jason.

Cheryl turned to me, a bit worried. "I don't know, Jared. We didn't talk about this."

"I know, I just thought of it."

"Wait a minute," said Darren. "You mean we all work together to really bother the unbeatables, and since no one knows about the club, they'll never be able to figure out who's doing it?"

"I love it!" said Abbie again.

"Classic!"

"Intense!"

"Jared, we could get in lots of trouble," said Cheryl.

"Naah," I said. "It's just for fun. We won't hurt anyone, we'll just bug the heck out of 'em!" Now everyone was walking around thinking about it. "You should be glad," I whispered to her. "I just saved your club."

She didn't say anything back, because she knew it was true.

Darren looked at me and smiled—almost in admiration. "This could be interesting," he said. "Maybe this is a good idea after all!"

If Cheryl hadn't been convinced before, that certainly convinced her.

"Of course it's a good idea!" said Cheryl.

"But wait," said Abbie. "What kind of tricks are we going to pull?"

"Well," I said, "let's sit down and think about it."

For an hour we brainstormed ideas, all the practical jokes you could think of! We laughed ourselves loony just imagining them. It was incredible! All seven of us working together toward a common goal. A club, a real club.

We all exchanged phone numbers, then everyone got up, climbed out of Stonehenge, and went their separate ways, leaving Cheryl and me alone. I grabbed the bucket of water I had brought to pour over the fire.

"They all had a great time!" said Cheryl.

"Yeah! It's like a real club."

"It *is* a real club. I can hardly wait till next week. Little Becky won't know what hit her!"

"Neither will Austin." Just imagining it gave me goose bumps all over. I felt so good, I could have gone over and given Cheryl a big hug for thinking of this club. I wanted to, but I didn't. Like I said, Cheryl and I were just friends.

I poured the bucket over the dying fire. It sizzled, a cloud of steam and smoke came billowing out, and then the fire was gone. That's when I realized how dark it was getting. I could barely see the walls of Stonehenge around us now.

"We're gonna have lots of fun, I think. You get some good ideas sometimes, Cheryl."

"You, too." And then she gave *me* a hug. I couldn't believe she did, but I was glad, so I hugged her back. For that split second, it felt like everything in the universe was perfect, and we were the center of it, down there in Stonehenge.

Then the feeling passed, and she let me go, and looked down. I didn't know what to do with my hands, so I put them in my pockets, and we stood there feeling incredibly dumb, listening to the sizzling of the dying fire.

"Hey," yelled Randall from the lip of Stonehenge. "Hey, are you coming or what, Cheryl? What are you guys doing down there anyway, making out?"

"Die!" said Cheryl.

"Yeah, sure. I know," he said. "Well, whatever you're doing, let's go or we'll be late for dinner."

"I'm coming."

She climbed out of Stonehenge, and I followed. Before I left, I turned back and watched the last bit of steam rise from the campfire, and smiled. Monday was going to be the start of a fantastic week!

Spiders and Snakes

I CAN'T SAY we didn't have fun. We did. We had lots of fun, and the fact that the members of the club were the only ones in on it made it that much more exciting. They were nasty tricks we pulled—we knew that all along—but we felt the victims deserved whatever they got. Our plans were so clever, so ingenious, that it seemed we could never get caught. You see, we pulled tricks for each other: Darren pulled Cheryl's trick on Rebecca, I pulled Randall's trick on Drew, and so on. That way it would be hard to figure out who was responsible; after all, what possible reason would I have for pulling a trick on Drew Landers? I could get away with it because I wasn't even a suspect! Working as a team made it hard for anyone—even us, sometimes—to figure out just who was doing what to whom. I guess every nightmare has to start somewhere. Ours started here.

Lunchtime. Tuesday. It was raining, so everyone was crammed into the cafeteria, which still had the faint smell of smoke from the small fire the week before. Cousin Rebecca was getting a present today, but only the members of the Shadow Club knew about it, and we all watched, scattered across the room, so as not to look suspicious, patiently waiting for Rebecca to open that ridiculous lunch box with teddy bears all over it.

Darren had taken care of this particular trick, so the rest of us knew what to expect, but weren't exactly sure when to expect it. Rebecca was all smiles, singing songs from *Annie* to herself and friends because she had gotten the lead role. Then she turned to open her lunch box. Nothing happened. I looked around the room. All eyes of the Shadow Club were focused on her. She talked a little bit more, and reached into her lunch box, pulling out the little plastic container that held her sandwich. I grimaced, preparing myself.

Nothing.

She opened the sandwich box, and pulled out a wedge of a gooey-looking peanut butter sandwich. She opened her bag of chips. Nothing. She laughed and sang, and porked out on her peanut butter sandwich—and then she reached for the thermos.

Oh no! I thought to myself. The thermos! Oh, how terrible! How marvelously, wonderfully terrible. I looked over toward Darren, and knew that this had to be it, for a smile had crept over his face.

Rebecca unscrewed the cap to the thermos and tilted its

open end toward the cup in her hand. A small green garter snake slithered its way out of the thermos into the cup, and then through sweet-little-Becky's fingers.

It took Rebecca a few moments to scream. I mean, how often do you expect a snake to come out of your thermos? It took about three seconds, then the thermos went flying, the snake went flying, and Rebecca let out a bloodcurdling scream that sounded five times as loud in the tiled cafeteria as it would have outside.

It didn't stop there. The snake landed on another table, and everyone there began to scream. Off it went into the air again, landing on some poor guy's sandwich, and his table began to scream. That poor little snake made it halfway around the cafeteria that day, and before long, people who didn't even know what was going on were screaming as well.

Rebecca continued to wail with a voice that kind of sounded like the way she sang, then, as she tended to do whenever life got the better of her, she began to suck her thumb—but her eyes went wide when she realized that the particular thumb she was sucking on had touched the snake. Out came the thumb and the screaming began once more.

As the chaos grew in the cafeteria, Cheryl came up to me and whispered to me.

"Isn't revenge sweet?" she said, and it certainly was. The Shadow Club was off to a flying start.

Vera Donaldson, the most popular girl in school, had a diary that she talked about, but never, ever brought to school. She also had a nine-year-old brother, and, as everyone knows, nine-year-old brothers can be bribed.

With Randall as mastermind, we found ourselves sitting in the middle of Stonehenge, with Vera Donaldson's diary sitting there with us.

"This is scary," said Jason. "It's like we got some sort of bible with us."

Randall smiled. "Vera's entire life is in this book."

"Dare we wreck it?" asked Cheryl, and everyone screamed, "Yes! Yes!"

We handed the diary to Abbie, and she read all about Vera's little life (which really did sound like a soap opera), until we came across a juicy bit of information that was just the sort of thing we were looking for.

When the meeting was over, Randall and Cheryl took the diary to the nearest copy shop and brought along their collection of dimes. By dinnertime the diary was back in the hands of Vera's little brother, and she never knew it was missing.

When morning came, everything was ready. All of us arrived super early to put up the papers around school. Nobody suspected.

Vera arrived at school, and was greeted by a piece of

paper taped to the front entrance that said the following, in her unmistakable handwriting:

> *Dear Diary,*
>
> *It's getting worse. I see him every day, and I want to talk to him, but I can't. I don't think he likes me. I'm sure he doesn't. I'll bet he thinks I like all those guys that keep asking me out.*
>
> *I love the clothes he wears, and I love the way he talks, but he never talks to me. I love his hair-style, and you know, he really has grown taller over the summer, I'm sure of it.*
>
> *I can't tell anyone, Diary, because they'll all think I'm nuts, but I think I'm in love with Martin Bricker, and I don't know what to do.*

I was there when Vera saw it. She didn't scream, she just sort of moaned in disbelief. Other kids had seen it already—half the school had read it. Vera tore the page down, and ripped it up, but as she went in, she saw the same piece of paper on every single classroom door in the school.

Everybody stared at her.

"Martin?" they sneered. "*You* like *Martin?*"

Even Tyson McGaw laughed at her—and if Tyson laughs at you, you know you're in trouble.

Vera, you see, was a ninth grader. And Martin was an eighth grader—a *short* eighth grader. If ever in history there were two people *not* meant to be together, these were the two.

Vera's face turned red, although it was hard to see it beneath all of that makeup, and she ran into the girls' bathroom, where she stayed till at least third period.

Martin Bricker, on the other hand, was in heaven all day.

Just as Jason Perez had told us, David Berger and his silver trumpet got all the solos in band, and he was always called to play with the high school band. At this weekend's high school football game, he had a solo that neither he, nor anyone sitting in front of him, would ever forget.

It was a simple enough plan that O.P. had thought up, but it would have been easy to get caught there in broad daylight, under the bleachers. O.P. had a lot more guts than anyone ever gave her credit for.

The band had warmed up and gotten ready to play. Jason told us that once their first march started, David wouldn't play a note until his solo came up, and that was perfect.

After warming up, David put his trumpet down next to him. He didn't notice when it was pulled away underneath the bleachers a moment later, and then returned to the exact spot where he had left it.

The song began, David stood up for his solo, blew into

his mouthpiece, and a whole containerful of green slime poured out of the other end. It was just the kind of green slime you could buy in any toy store, but that didn't matter; it was disgusting, and that's all that anyone cared about. The bandleader and half the football team stared at David in amazement.

David, still unsure of what was going on, blew harder into his trumpet, and the green slime blew out of the end and all over the band. As far as the band was concerned, this was the end of the world. They all began to yell and run out of his way as David blew into the trumpet again, sending slime flying, this time along with a dull tone from the trumpet that sounded pretty rude. In ten seconds the band had cleared out and was running to the locker rooms to get out of their slimed outfits, leaving David alone, his face turning red as he continued to slime the bleachers.

The next trick, by far, was the most dangerous. I was there, because it was my turn to pull a prank. Cheryl and Randall came along to watch.

Midnight. Wednesday. We stood outside Drew Landers' open bedroom window.

"Maybe we ought to think of another trick," said Cheryl. The lights were out in the house, and we were sure Drew was asleep, but still . . .

"No way!" said Randall. "This is perfect! Perfect! We

have to do it. Trust me, Drew can sleep through anything! Once, he fell asleep in math, and they couldn't wake him up! They had to call in the nurse!"

Cheryl turned to me. "If you still want to do it, then I'm with you."

I smiled, and carefully removed the screen, then climbed in through the open window.

Drew Landers' room was a mess. I mean, I've seen my room get pretty scary, but this was a pigsty. It was hard to walk without stepping on things that crunched.

Drew slept under a mass of covers in his bed. We could hear him snoring more loudly than the roar of the filter on the huge fish aquarium in the corner.

"Look at this," whispered Randall, pointing to a whole row of swimming trophies on a shelf above the aquarium. Cheryl put her finger to her lips to shut him up.

Drew did not hear a thing. He continued snoring as I very carefully rolled the covers away from his feet. He was wearing dirty socks. Moving a fraction of an inch per second, I peeled back the socks until his feet, which smelled a little like chlorine and a little like vinegar, were sticking straight up at me. I reached my hand out to Cheryl, and she handed me the nail polish.

When Drew woke up in the morning, just as we had thought, he didn't change his socks, and fifteen hours after we had left his house, an incredibly embarrassed Drew Landers had to explain to the entire swim team why his toenails were painted red.

Eric Kilfoil, the basketball star, was a sweater. Not the kind you wear, but the kind that drips all over the floor during a basketball game. Antiperspirant didn't help his sweating problem very much, but, as Darren told us, Eric would always roll on a sizable helping of antiperspirant under his arms before going out onto the court.

The trick that Abbie planned turned out to be much more complicated than it sounded, because, not only did we have to switch antiperspirant bottles, but we also had to make sure that Eric never saw what he was coating his armpits with. In the end, we had to black out the locker room at the perfect moment, just to keep Eric, and the rest of the basketball team, in the dark as to what was going on.

We were all there in the stands when the basketball team came out of the dark locker room and into the gym. Darren looked up from the floor and gave us the "OK" sign.

The team wore their warm-ups through the layup drills. Finally, when the game was about to start, the warm-ups came off, revealing the team uniforms. Eric's was already beginning to look sweaty.

It was jump ball, and, of course, Eric jumped. His arm went up, and in the excitement, nobody noticed Eric's underarms but the referee. The whistle dropped out of his mouth.

The other team had possession of the ball, and Eric ran down the court, taking his position as center of the 2-1-2 zone. His arms went up, and that's when everyone else saw it: fluorescent green sweat under his arms, soaking the sides of his shirt!

Well, the captain of the other team dribbled the ball through the defense, then stopped dead when he saw Eric's little problem.

"Hey, what's with the armpits, dude?" said the kid with the ball.

Now, when somebody says something about your armpits, you have to look; you can't help it, even if you're in the middle of a basketball game. Eric reached under his left arm and came out with a fluorescent green hand. The kid shot a basket over Eric's head to score.

Had the joke ended there, we would have been more than satisfied—but it didn't.

We didn't count on Eric being color-blind.

"I'm bleeding!" cried Eric, stumbling around the court, showing everybody his very green hands. "I'm bleeding! I'm bleeding!" The game sort of stopped as everyone tried to figure out if this could be possible. If it was, Eric must have been an alien. "Help, I'm bleeding, I'm bleeding!" he cried. "Call the nurse!"

And everyone was so confused and dumbfounded by this weird turn of events that the nurse was called immediately.

The most obnoxious of our tricks was a doubleheader. It involved two kids, and one of them was L'Austin Space.

You see, Mr. Milburn, the science teacher, had a collection of animals in his classroom. Animals that ranged from gerbils to lizards. Tommy Nickols, the ninth grade's foremost brain, kept his pride and joy in Mr. Milburn's room: Octavia, his beloved pet tarantula. Sometime after lunch, Tommy noticed that Octavia was missing, but try as he might, he could not seem to find her. She was not in her cage, she was not hiding in the bookshelf. It seemed she was nowhere in the room, and nobody could find her.

L'Austin Space found her. Or should I say that *she* found *him?*

I was particularly mad at Austin that day, so I couldn't wait to see the trick pulled off. You see, Austin had called me Gopher so much that everyone had started to call me that. I couldn't wait to get back at him.

Anyway, it was a rainy day, and so Austin, as well as everyone else, came to school in a hooded jacket. In homeroom, at the end of the day, everyone put on their coats and waited for the bell to ring. Ralphy Sherman saw it first.

"Hey, Austin," he said, "there's something in your hood!"

"Yeah, sure," said Austin, because nobody ever believed a word Ralphy said.

"If there was something in my hood, would I do this?" And Austin, thinking himself pretty clever, put his hood on. When he pulled his hood off again, a tarantula was sitting on his head.

"AHHH!" he screamed, running around the room. "Get it off me! Get it off me!"

He wouldn't touch it. The thing was sitting smack on the middle of his head, but he was too grossed out to actually touch it. Well, just like with the snake, everybody in the room, including Mrs. Marlow, our homeroom teacher, began to scream. Meanwhile, Austin ran around the room with Tommy Nickols running behind him, crying, "Don't hurt her! Don't hurt Octavia! She doesn't bite, she's a *good* tarantula."

However, when a tarantula is doing push-ups on your scalp, you don't care how good it is; you just want it off. Watching Austin turn white as a ghost was the high point of my day—and then, as if it wasn't bad enough, Octavia got freaked out and tried to climb off. Unfortunately, the easiest way off of Austin's head was down the back of his shirt.

Austin fell to the ground, shaking his shirt, but Octavia wouldn't come out. She'd had enough for one day.

Austin tore off his shirt, ripping out all the buttons, and Octavia went sailing across the room. When she landed she wasted no time in racing across the floor for a place to hide.

"Don't hurt her!" yelled Tommy Nickols. "She's tame, really, she's a *domesticated* spider!" But no one much cared. While most everyone stood on the tables, Octavia scampered around the room between the table legs, until she finally met an untimely end under the heel of Richard Fergusson's shoe.

L'Austin Space sat on the floor in a daze, for once actually lost in space. Tommy Nickols had collapsed to his knees in tears, mourning his dearly departed spider, and Richard Fergusson threw his shoe into the wastepaper basket, choosing to walk home barefoot.

Celebration at Stonehenge

IT WAS THE third Friday after the signing of the charter, and as usual, we met at Stonehenge. From the very beginning, the place seemed to have some mystical meaning for us; those moss-covered stones around the dark pit. Now there was even more meaning. It was our hideout, our special place—the only place where we could swap stories about who did what to whom, and how well the pranks worked. We celebrated our victories down in Stonehenge.

The rains had passed, the wind had brought down new firewood from the trees, and the sun had dried it off for us, so we had a good fire going by the time the sun fell low in the sky. As we talked, a big bag of marshmallows went around the circle until each marshmallow sat roasted in our stomachs.

"Did you see the look on Vera Donaldson's face as she went around tearing the copies of her diary down from the classroom doors?" asked Abbie.

"Classic," said Jason.

"You know, the next day," Cheryl added, "all the eighth graders started asking her out. I don't mean the big eighth graders, I mean the puny ones like Martin, that look like seventh graders! They figured that because she liked Martin, she must like younger guys! She nearly died of humiliation!"

"I love it," said Abbie, as she brushed her hair (which she did a lot).

"Wait, wait, wait!" said Darren. "If you want to talk about the look on someone's face, how about the second Austin realized there was a spider on his head!"

"Or the second it slipped down his shirt!" cried O.P.

"Classic!" said Jason.

"Intense!" said O.P.

"That spider was great, man," said Darren. "It's like the thing knew exactly what we wanted it to do!"

"I wish I could have seen it!" said Jason.

"We should make that spider an honorary member of the club," I said.

"Yeah. Too bad it's dead," said Darren, shoving a marshmallow into his mouth.

"You're all wrong!" said Randall. "The best—the absolute best thing ever, in the history of the whole world—was the look on Drew Landers' face as he took off his socks in the locker room, in front of the whole team—and none of you got to see it!" he said, gloating.

"Tell us about it!" said Abbie.

"OK," said Randall. Everyone in the club was listening. "The whole team was done changing except for Drew, when the coach passed through the locker room on his way to the pool. I started asking the coach questions to keep him there."

"You mean the coach was there, too?" asked Abbie.

"I'm getting to it!"

"I love it!" said Abbie.

"Anyway, the coach starts telling me that, as usual, I'm in all of Drew's races, and as usual, I knew he'd take first place. Then, just like I predicted, Drew takes off those filthy dirty socks. Jared—you did such a good job of painting his nails, it was incredible! I could have died! Anyway, Drew didn't notice it at first—he put his bathing suit on and didn't even see it—but the coach saw it."

"Oh, no!" I screamed. This was great!

"Classic!" cried Jason. "Classic. Just classic!"

"Shut up, let me finish. OK, so the coach sees him, toenails and all—they were fire-engine red—you couldn't miss them, and the coach just says, 'Drew? Your feet!' and everyone looks down at Drew's toes. Nobody laughs—everyone thought it was for real, you know, like Drew did it all by himself. Everybody's saying, 'Wow' and 'I don't believe it,' and stuff like that.

"Finally Drew looks at his feet, then he turns to the coach, his eyebrows and face all wrinkled up like he's about to sneeze, and he begins stuttering like this, 'I . . . I . . . I . . . duh . . . duh . . . duh.' He tries to hide his feet, and that's when the team starts to laugh. I swear those painted toes were the most ridiculous thing in the history of the planet!"

"I love it!"

"Classic!"

"Intense!"

"So anyway," continued Randall, "Drew can't get a word out he's so embarrassed, and then—get this—the coach starts laughing, too!"

At that, any of us who were holding back couldn't hold it any longer. We all began to laugh. Laughing our heads off because we humiliated Drew Landers. Kind of sick, huh?

When Randall regained control of his laughter he finished the story.

"This is the best part," said Randall. "While we all sat there, laughing at those stupid red toes, Drew Landers—Mr. Macho Swimmer himself—began to cry!"

"Yeah!" screamed Darren. "Revenge!"

"We all got our revenge!" said Cheryl. "And the more they humiliate us, the more revenge we're going to get!"

Everybody agreed. Even O.P.—shy O.P.—was all smiles there at the campfire. It seemed that beneath that quiet brainy exterior lurked a kid just like the rest of us, who just loved every minute of our little pranks.

"Hey, everybody," said O.P. "I'd like to read something to

you." All eyes turned to her as she pulled out a piece of paper. "As you know, David Berger—Jason's mortal enemy—
had green slime mysteriously loaded into his trumpet."
Everyone chuckled. "Well," she continued, "I would like to
read you this small poem that came out in the high school
paper this week—not junior high school, but high school!"

"We made the big time!" I said.

"Listen to this." She unfolded the newspaper clipping,
and began reading:

> *"The team was on the field,*
> *And vict'ry was at hand.*
> *Yes, everything seemed wonderful,*
> *Then David slimed the band.*
> *He did it with such style and grace,*
> *You'd think that it was planned.*
> *Not one musician got off clean,*
> *When David slimed the band.*
> *The flutes were sprayed with sticky goo,*
> *Their players filled with scorn.*
> *The bandleader got slimed on, too,*
> *When David blew his horn.*
> *The football players turned their heads,*
> *And heard the band all say,*
> *'There is no doubt, we are grossed out,'*
> *As they all ran away.*

Next week they'll all wear raincoats,
And gloves upon their hands.
Blame it all on one trumpet call,
When David slimed the band."

We were in stitches, laughing so hard our stomachs began to hurt. Ever have one of those laughing fits where one person's laughter keeps feeding the others, until nobody can stop? That's what it was like. Between the sliming, and the tarantula, and the nail polish, and the diary, and the snake, and the green blood, it was just too much for any group of human beings to handle. We just had to laugh and laugh.

Finally, about five minutes later, we came down off of our laughing fit, wheezing, and wiping our eyes dry. The fire had now become full and furious, sending sparks sailing into the dimming sky. We all relaxed, and I found that somehow during the laughing fit, I had ended up leaning back, my head resting comfortably in Cheryl's lap. I looked up at her, and she smiled at me. She was playing with my hair. The strangest thing about it was that I did not feel uncomfortable at all!

"This is classic," said Jason, and although he said that quite a lot, we knew exactly what he meant. Even though most of us had barely known each other three weeks ago, right now, at this one moment in time, we would all agree that we were the best friends in the world.

I looked up at Cheryl, whose hair was dangling just an inch above my nose, and smiled.

That's when I heard it. We all heard it. I snapped up out of Cheryl's lap, and we all turned our heads to listen.

"What was that?" asked Randall.

"Shhhh!" Cheryl said.

We all listened, and heard it again, the scraping of branches, the crunching of leaves. Something was out there, just above the pit, on the other side of Stonehenge. We were all thinking the same thing. No one ever saw any bears in these woods, but Ralphy Sherman swore that once Bigfoot came up to him and then ran away. Of course, Ralphy Sherman also swore that he was picked up by one-eyed aliens, taken to a distant galaxy, and returned in time for evening television, so no one much trusted Ralphy Sherman—still, you never really know. There were also stories of a mountain lion who was shot by a family hiking only thirty miles away. None of us had any weapons. There were deer in the woods, but what if it wasn't a deer?

We were all silent, and could still hear the faintest movement just a few feet away. I sniffed the air—perhaps if it was some large animal I could smell it—but all I could smell was the smoke from the fire. And then I said the stupidest thing that has ever been uttered by anybody on the face of this earth.

"I'll go check."

Nobody else volunteered. I slowly stood and walked over to the dirt slope where one corner of Stonehenge had caved in dozens of years ago, and I made my way up.

Now, on the other side of Stonehenge, I was all alone, and for all I knew this could have been the end of my life. Still, I forced myself on, because waiting there in the middle like a sitting duck wouldn't do any of us any good. I walked around Stonehenge, and I heard it again! Moving branches! There was no mistaking it, something was up here, just around the corner of the old stone foundation. My heart began to beat faster. If I could just get a glimpse of it before it saw me, I'd be all right. If it were a deer, then fine, I would go back down, case closed. If it were something worse, I could warn everyone and we could scatter—we'd have better chances that way. Of course, if we scattered, the thing would probably go after me first, since I was right there, but I wasn't about to start thinking things like that.

I neared the stone corner, and slowly peered around. Trees, trees, and more trees came into view, until I saw something at the far end turning a corner. It wasn't a deer. It wasn't Bigfoot. It was a kid. I saw his back and feet as he turned the corner, but did not see his face. Whoever it was had been watching us, and had heard our secrets; knew exactly what we had done, and what was going on! If someone knew, then our whole club could be destroyed! I was not about to allow that!

"Everybody hurry up here, some kid's been watching us!"

Everyone stood, and raced up and out of Stonehenge.

"This way," I yelled. I rounded the next corner, and saw him again, this time disappearing into the woods. He was trying to get away, the little spy!

"Is there only one of them?" asked Cheryl.

"I think so."

"If he tells, we're in lots of trouble!"

"I know."

The Shadow Club raced through the woods, and as our eyes began to adjust to the dim light, we could see him just twenty feet in front of us. I raced at full speed. He was nearing the road!

At last I got close enough, and dove on him, bringing him down. He was about my size, just a bit skinnier. A bit bonier. I rolled him over and looked at the face before me. I instantly knew who it was, and so did the rest of the Shadow Club.

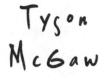

GET YOUR HANDS off me, you idiot!" yelled Tyson.

"Oh my gosh, it's the slimeball!" said Darren. "Now we're in for it!"

"What were you doing up there?" I demanded, pinning his shoulders to the ground as hard as I could.

"Get off me, butt head, you're hurting me!"

"I asked you a question!"

"You're hurting me!"

"Good!" said Abbie. "He'll hurt you more if you don't tell!" Tyson didn't say a word.

"I'm warning you, Tyson, we have ways of making you talk—and you won't like any of them."

"I didn't see anything."

"Bull," said Randall.

"Bring him back to Stonehenge!" said O.P.

"To Stonehenge," echoed the rest. "Yes, bring him back to Stonehenge," and that's just what we did. I put him in a full nelson. He struggled, but Darren grabbed his feet, and we carried him back through the woods, to Stonehenge.

The fire was still at full blaze when we carried Tyson down into the stone foundation. He had stopped struggling some time ago. We let him go, and he stood, his back against the wall, with all seven of us standing in front of him.

"What is this, a gang?" asked Tyson. I thought about that for a second, but let it fly out the other ear.

"There's seven of us, Tyson," I said, "and only one of you. You had better tell us what you saw."

"I wouldn't tell you if you were the last person on earth!"

"Beat him up!" yelled Jason, standing in the background, pounding his fist into his other hand. "Make him talk!"

"Yeah!" yelled O.P.

"No!" I said. I could see that being rough with Tyson just made him clam up even more. We needed a different approach.

"Listen, Tyson," I said. "We don't want to hurt you, or anything. We're all friends, right?"

"No," said Abbie.

"I said we're all friends . . . *right?*"

Everyone reluctantly agreed.

"Now, why don't you tell us what you saw?" I backed up a little bit, giving Tyson some room. He looked around at us, and seemed a bit less angry—although that crazy look he had in his eyes never went away. He looked at us for a long time, and then said:

"All I saw was you guys laughing. That's all. I saw you laughing for a long time. That's all."

"You expect us to believe that?" said Cheryl.

"It's the truth!"

"Then why did you run!" demanded Darren.

"I don't know. Because you started chasing me. That's why."

"We chased you because you were spying on us," I said.

"Well, I just wanted to find out what you were laughing about, OK? That's all." Tyson looked at us all with that mean, dark look in his eyes, then hung his head. "I just wanted to find out . . . because I thought that maybe you were talking about me, and that's why you were laughing."

"Why would we talk about you?" asked Cheryl.

"Because people talk about me. I hear it. They think I don't, but I do. They laugh at me all the time, and call me slimeball. Anyway, that's all I saw. Laughing."

"We don't believe you," said Cheryl.

I sort of half believed him and half didn't. "What are you doing around here anyway?" I asked.

"I live near here . . . down that way," he pointed.

"You're lying," said Randall. "There are no houses around here."

"There's one," said Tyson. "On the cliff, by the ocean."

"The lighthouse?" said Jason.

"It's not a lighthouse anymore. I live there."

Everyone was quiet for a while. Nobody knew what to say next. If Tyson was lying, there was nothing we could do about it. He'd never tell the truth, no matter what we did to him.

"All right," I said. "I don't care what you saw, or what you heard, but I'll tell you one thing; if you so much as tell another living soul that you saw us all here, you'll be sorry. Do you swear never to tell anyone?"

Tyson looked down. "Maybe."

"No maybes."

"All right—but on one condition."

"What?"

Tyson looked at me, and for a very brief instant, I saw something else besides that stupid-crazy look in Tyson's eyes. I don't know exactly what it was that I saw, but it was kind of like what you see when you look into a baby's eyes, and Tyson said, "I swear I won't tell a soul . . . if you let me in your gang."

"*What?*"

"Please, I've never been in a gang before. I'll do a good job—a great job—just let me in your gang."

"It's not a gang!" I screamed into his face, and shook him as hard as I could. "You don't know a thing!"

And then Tyson changed again. The craziness was back.

"Well, to hell with you!" he said. "All of you! I don't want to be in a gang of bullies, and you're the biggest bully of them all!"

"I'm not a bully!" I screamed at him, then pushed him back against the wall as hard as I could. If there was one thing in this world that I was not, it was that. I was not a bully! I grabbed him and pushed him against the wall again, to make my point clear.

Then Randall went up to him. Randall was a year younger and four inches shorter than Tyson, but that didn't matter. Randall went right up to him, and grabbed the front of his shirt, and wrinkled it in his fist. He got really close to Tyson, and snarled at him in a way that I'd never heard Randall snarl.

"Your life isn't worth much if you breathe a word of this to anyone, you stupid slimeball." We all waited a moment, and then, out of nowhere, Randall spat in Tyson's face. "That's what you get for spying, sleazebag."

The fight had left Tyson. He looked down, wiping his face, and mumbled, "You didn't have to do that."

Cheryl and I stared at Randall as he backed off. Randall looked at us and shrugged. I tried not to think about what Randall had just done.

"Can I do that, too?" asked Jason. No one answered him.

"Why don't you go home, Tyson?" I said. "And forget you ever saw us. For your own good."

Tyson turned, mumbled something nasty under his breath, and left.

The fire needed more wood, but no one felt like feeding it. It was dark now, and our parents were probably beginning to wonder where we were. No one felt much like talking after Tyson left, and so a few minutes later, the meeting broke up. Cheryl and Randall waited as I poured water on the fire.

"So what's next for the Shadow Club?" asked Cheryl. I stepped up out of Stonehenge, then reached out my hand, and helped Cheryl. I never did let go of her hand after she was out—and strangely enough, I didn't seem to care. I didn't even care if Randall noticed that we were holding hands—which he didn't. Although it was starting to get chilly, Cheryl's hand was soft and warm, and it felt good to hold it.

"What's next?" I said. "I don't know. More tricks maybe?"

"Maybe."

"We used all the good ones," said Randall. "How can we top those?"

"I don't know," I said. "Why don't we think about it, then we'll all talk at our next meeting."

"Are you worried about Tyson telling everyone?" Cheryl asked.

"Aren't you?"

"Yeah."

"What can we do to him if he tells?" asked Randall.

"I don't know," I said.

As we walked back through the woods, I was certainly glad that Cheryl's hands were warm. Because mine kept getting colder.

Two hours later, at 8:00, I left my house again. I told my parents that I was going over to Cheryl's to work on a science project. Since I never lied to them, and I had always been pretty responsible and trustworthy, they believed me and let me go. Needless to say, there was no science project, and I had no intention of going to Cheryl's house. I would have liked to, but I had some important business to take care of.

I began running at a slow pace. I ran past Cheryl's house, and past all the houses on the street. I ran to the edge of the neighborhood, and then down the road that passed by Stonehenge. I could have taken the shortcut through the woods, but I didn't feel like doing that at night.

I ran for about a mile, which was not hard for me, and then saw what I was looking for. At the edge of the woods, on a wide grassy knoll, stood the old lighthouse. A small wooden home had been built around the old stone tower, and no light had shone in that tower for maybe a hundred years. It only made sense to me that Tyson lived in a lighthouse with no light.

I was curious about Tyson and the mysterious secrets I had heard so many rumors about, secrets of his past and of his family. I was not there because I was curious, though; I was there for a reason. If I could find a secret—any secret— about Tyson, then I could bargain with him. I wouldn't tell his secret, if he didn't tell about the Shadow Club. It was a simple enough plan, but finding the secret was not going to be easy.

My hair is blond, and easy to see, so as I got closer, I pulled the black hood of my sweat jacket over my head.

As I approached Tyson's house, I began to get a bit frightened, thinking about all the things I had heard in the three years that Tyson had lived in town. Some said that Tyson lived with his aunt and uncle—that's what Tyson said—but we weren't quite sure. Someone heard that they were actually foster parents. But whatever they were, one thing was certain: Tyson didn't live with his real parents, and no one knew why. There were dozens of rumors about that. Some said that they had abandoned Tyson on a street corner, some said that they were dead, and some said they beat Tyson, and were in jail. Ralphy Sherman said that they were a family of ax murderers and hid out in the woods somewhere, but then, Ralphy Sherman also said that he went skydiving without a parachute on Sundays, so no one put much faith in the ax-murderer story—still, you never know.

Anyway, those were the thoughts that were toying with my mind as I got closer to Tyson's remodeled lighthouse.

It wasn't much of a house. It was like a small shack, built right up on the edge of the cliff, attached to the lighthouse. It was small but well kept.

Keeping myself low, I made my way to the side of the house, and peered into a window. Two people who seemed on the verge of being elderly sat on a couch watching TV. I stood there for a few minutes. Tyson was not there, and these people—who must have been Tyson's "aunt and uncle," or whatever—did not move from the couch at all.

They're dead, said a voice in my brain that sounded a bit like Ralphy Sherman. *They're dead, and they've been stuffed!*

Just then, the woman mumbled something about how many commercials were on the tube nowadays. So much for them being stuffed.

I ducked again and made my way around the side, just by the edge of the cliff. Again I looked into a window. This time I had found Tyson's room. It was small, with just enough room for a bed and a desk, and Tyson was sitting at his desk, working on something. For some reason, I sort of expected Tyson's room to be like that. There was a second window, overlooking the ocean, and the far wall was bare except for a single picture, smack in the middle. The framed photo was of a kid who looked an awful lot like Tyson, but younger, standing with a man and a woman—definitely not the people who now sat in the living room. This must have been Tyson with his real parents.

What I saw on the other wall seemed completely out of place. Hanging from hooks on the wall were puppets—or not puppets, but marionettes—little dolls with carved hands and feet and drawn faces, hanging by dozens of strings. I knew for a fact that those kinds of things were expensive, but Tyson had lots of them. Then I saw another one, sitting on Tyson's desk next to a mess of wood, plastic, fabric, and knives that Tyson was fiddling with. That's when it hit me that Tyson had made these! I looked back at the ones hanging by the wall. Each had a different face and wore different clothes. There was one with loud clothes, wild hair, and big breasts that kind of looked like Abbie. One with red hair and white shoes that kind of looked like Austin, and one with blond hair that I swear looked kind of like me. I mean, I knew it was all a coincidence, right? Still it was creepy all the same.

So, Tyson made puppets. Could that be a big enough secret, I thought? Naah. I needed something bigger. Something that would shut Tyson's mouth up like a clam. I stood there outside, peeping into Tyson's window, then the living room window, then the kitchen window, waiting for something. I knew spying like that was a low-down thing to do, but I had to do it for the good of the club. I tried to think of myself as 007, instead of as a Peeping Tom.

After twenty minutes, I began to worry that perhaps this was not going to work. Maybe Tyson's secrets were so well hidden I would never find them.

And then Tyson's "aunt" said something.

"Ty," she said, "did you make your bed this morning?"

"There weren't any clean sheets," said Tyson from the other room.

"There are now. Make your bed."

Now, this might seem strange to you, but I had a feeling about this one, a really good feeling. Quickly I made my way around to Tyson's room. He was gone, but in a moment, he came in with a sheet. He put it on the chair and pulled back his bedspread to make the bed.

In one instant, I knew everything I needed to know about Tyson McGaw.

"How ya doin', Gopher?" said L'Austin. He had just done his morning laps and was ready to do his sprint on the grass, when I crossed the field toward school on Monday. The "Gopher" business was getting way out of hand, and we both knew it. Not only had the entire team decided my new name was Gopher, but half the school was now calling me that, and it was getting worse. Some kids didn't even know my real name; I was just the Gopher. It was enough to make me want to quit the team, but that was just what Austin wanted, and I wasn't about to let him get the better of me.

"What are you smiling about?" asked Austin. "Get faster over the weekend?"

"Maybe," I said, smiling.

"You better be on time for practice today," he said, "or else I'll make you do extra laps."

"What are you, coach now?" I asked, still smiling.

"Coach, captain, what's the difference? The point is, you gotta listen to what I say, right?"

The smile was leaving my face quickly.

"See you later, Gopher." He blasted off barefoot across the grass, moving faster than any ninth grader in the world except for me should be able to run.

"Watch that you don't run into any friendly spiders, Austin!" I yelled after him. He stumbled for a moment, but kept on running.

As I left the field I passed his stupid white Aeropeds resting in the grass. A month into school, and they were still as white as snow. Stupid shoes. Well, who cared about Austin? I had a mission that morning, and I was not about to let old Tarantula-head spoil it.

Off I marched into the building and waited by my locker for a sign of Tyson McGaw.

"Get out of my face!" said Tyson. I was standing right next to him as he opened his locker. The second the door opened I pushed it shut.

"That's no way to talk, Tyson."

"All right," said Tyson. "Get out of my face, *moron*."

"I'm not in your face, I'm standing next to you. Do you have problems judging distance? Is that it?"

"Just leave me alone." Tyson opened his locker and put his books in.

"I just wanted to tell you something, Tyson."

"Yeah, like what?"

"I just wanted to say that I like the puppets on your wall." Tyson snapped his head to me. That crazy look in his eyes became fuller.

"What do you know about it?"

"I saw them. I looked through your window one night, and I saw them."

"You're lying!"

"Why would I lie, Tyson? Besides, how else would I know about them?"

Tyson said nothing. He just stared at me.

"Is that what you do all the time, make puppets?" I asked.

"Is that all you do, look in people's windows?" he said. "Anyway, it's none of your business, and you'd better not look in my window anymore!"

"Why not? Got something to hide, Tyson?"

"You just better not, that's all."

"You spied on us, so I just spied back on you. There's also something else I know about you, Tyson."

"What?"

And staring straight at him I said, "I know that you're a bed wetter."

Suddenly that crazy look in his eyes became even more frightening than I thought it could. It was as if Tyson's eyes were a window to some dark, horrible place that only he knew about. It was like his eyes could have turned me to stone.

"That's a lie," he snarled, like a caged animal would snarl.

"I saw, Tyson. I watched you change your sheets. I saw the stains on them. I saw the rubber sheet. I know all about you, Tyson."

"It's not true!" he growled.

I didn't say anything.

"I hate you!" he yelled. Then, softer: "You better not tell anyone, because if you do . . ."

"Quiet!" I said. "All right, I'll make a deal with you. If you don't tell anyone about the Shadow Club, I won't tell anyone about your rubber sheets. Is it a deal? C'mon, is it?"

Tyson stared at me, unable to speak. His frightening, empty eyes got deeper, then suddenly it was like the bottom dropped out of his mind. He bared his teeth, snarled, and lunged at me, grabbing my hair and my throat, fighting like no normal kid fights. In a second, dozens of kids were all around watching—most laughing at Tyson, like they always laughed.

"I'll kill you if you tell," he screamed. "Killyou-killyou-killyou-killyou!" I pushed him away, but he came right back at me. Maybe I should have been punching him back, I don't know. I guess I felt it was unfair to hit him, so I just kept pushing him off me, and he kept lunging, with tears in those wolf eyes.

Finally, Vice Principal Greene came running down the hall and grabbed Tyson, shaking him and talking to him as if he were trying to shake someone out of a bad nightmare. Eventually Tyson snapped back into sanity.

"What is this all about?" Mr. Greene asked me. I shrugged. "Nothing," I said. "He just came at me. I think I must have bumped into his locker."

And Mr. Greene believed me, because I was always such a good kid who never caused anyone any problems. It scared me to think what I could get away with if I really wanted to. It scared me and bothered me to think of how I was toying with poor Tyson's head, so I tried not to think about it.

"All right, Tyson, why don't you tell me why you went after him?"

Tyson just looked at him, then at me, with his jaw open, as if he would spill out the whole story. Then finally he looked down.

"He bumped into my locker," said Tyson.

"Fine. Let's have a talk in my office, Tyson," said Mr. Greene. He looked at the crowd in the hallway. "Didn't I just hear the homeroom bell? Don't you all have somewhere to go?"

The crowd began to break up, and Greene walked with Tyson down the hall. Tyson turned back to look at me, both of us realizing that I had him over a barrel, and there was nothing he could do about it. I winked at him, and he threw back at me that stone-turning gaze of his.

I guess in some ways I *had* turned to stone, but it wasn't by Tyson. It was by the Shadow Club.

The Best of Friends

A **S USUAL, MOST** of us pretended not to know each other at school that week. Sure, Cheryl and I hung around together, but as far as the rest of the club went, well, we just winked at each other in the halls. The secrecy of our friendships made the meetings at Stonehenge very special.

By next Friday's meeting, however, I was feeling awfully strange about things. Tyson hadn't spilled the beans to anyone, as far as I knew, and none of us had gotten caught for any of the practical jokes we had played, but still something didn't sit quite right. Maybe it was the feeling I'd got when I told Tyson I knew he was a bed wetter. Maybe it was the fact that I had to spy on him like a Peeping Tom. Or maybe it was the fact that Tyson had called us a gang. Whatever it was, I took the feeling to the meeting with me, and I couldn't shake it. I held my hands close to the fire. It seemed that for the past few meetings nothing I could do would keep my hands warm.

"You know," said Darren, "I never thought this thing would work. I mean, I never thought we'd all actually . . . you know, *like* each other."

"I'll say," said Abbie. "Look at this group: we've got a jock, a brain, a nerd, a sōsh, a brat, a lawyer, and the Gopher! Who'd have thought we'd all get along!"

I smiled, but down inside I cringed. The kids in the Shadow Club were the only ones in school left who *didn't* call me the Gopher.

"I'm not a jock!" said Darren.

"And I'm not a nerd!" said Jason.

"Yeah, but you know what I mean," said Abbie.

I knew what she meant. Except for Randall, Cheryl, and me, none of us had really known each other before the club.

"I guess when you have something in common," said O.P., "it's easy to be friends." Oh, yeah, sure, we really had a lot in common, I thought.

"We all hate somebody," I said.

O.P. turned to me. "What?"

"We hate somebody. That's all we have in common. A little bit sick, huh?"

"Naah," said Darren. "It's like war. Common enemies bring people close, you know?"

"But we're not at war," I said.

"Yeah, we are," said Jason. "We're fighting for our right not to be humiliated by the unbeatables."

"I say we nuke 'em!" said Randall.

"And I say that's not funny!" I yelled. I wondered which was worse, wanting to nuke somebody, or wishing someone was never born. There were seven of us, all wishing that seven other people in the world had never been brought into it. That's the kind of hatred you read about in war books; the kind of hate that kills millions of people.

Everyone around the circle looked at me as if I had cussed Randall out.

"I think you're taking this all too seriously, Jared," said Cheryl. "It's just for fun."

"I think he's feeling guilty," said Abbie.

"What for?" said Darren. "Our jokes didn't hurt anybody, did they? I mean, sure a spider got killed, but I kill spiders every day. Do you see me crying about it?"

He had a good point, but it didn't make me feel any better. I took my hands away from the fire. Almost immediately, they began to get cold again, but when I put my hands down, Cheryl grabbed one of them and held it gently, out of everyone's view. That's when I began to feel a bit better about everything.

"I think I know what it is," said O.P. "I think he's worried about Tyson talking."

"No! That's not it," I said, and took a deep breath.

"You want out of the club? Is that it?" asked Darren.

"No, of course not. I like the club—I love the club . . . but . . ."

"But what?" said Darren. "Get to the point."

"Maybe we should stop the tricks," I said.

Cheryl turned to me. "Jared, our charter is based on revenge."

"Yeah," said Randall. "The tricks were your idea. Don't wimp out on us, Jared."

"Yeah, Jared," echoed Jason.

"Hasn't it been great fun so far?" asked Abbie. I thought about it. It *had* been great fun.

"And didn't everyone deserve what they got?" asked O.P. She was right. They all deserved what they got.

"And don't you enjoy being president of the club?" asked Cheryl. She hooked me with that one, and that's when any guilt or doubt I had inside switched off completely. Until that moment, I had never thought of myself as president, but as I looked around the fire, I saw that everyone was looking at me—not just looking at me, but looking up to me—*me*, the Generic Kid, who never stood out in a crowd, and whose face nobody could remember.

What an idiot I had been! Here I was, the leader of this club, and I was on the verge of throwing it all away. I wasn't about to do that.

"Maybe what we need is a slight change of club policy," said Cheryl. I knew what she meant; I picked right up on it. Keep my voice firm; no more wishy-washiness. If I was the president, then I was going to tell them how the club was going to work.

"All right," I said in my power voice, "if we're going to keep this club from falling apart—or even worse, from getting caught—we have to stop the tricks for a while."

Randall and a few of the others whined.

"Quiet!" I said. "I'm not finished." I couldn't believe how quickly they stopped whining. I held back a smile. We were in charge, both Cheryl and I; we had power, and my voice didn't crack once! "We have to stop the tricks, and only pull them once in a while—when we really feel somebody deserves it. That way, we can give them exactly what they deserve, *when* they deserve it, and we'll never get caught! That's our new policy, right, Cheryl?"

"Right!" Cheryl smiled, and held my hand a bit tighter.

Everyone looked at each other for a few moments, then Abbie said, "That makes perfect sense to me," and everyone agreed; even Darren.

"What do we do in the meantime?" he asked.

"Eat more marshmallows." Cheryl tossed him the bag.

"OK," said Darren, and he did just that.

After that, everything lightened up. Cheryl and I were in charge. Everyone knew it, and everyone accepted it. For the rest of the afternoon, we talked about everything from the fires at school to whether or not anything Ralphy Sherman ever said in his whole life was true. It was great, for, as Cheryl said sometime during that afternoon, we were a bunch of kids—not a gang—having fun without doing anything wrong (or at least we weren't doing anything wrong at that moment). We were good kids, with good grades, from good homes. Everything about us was good, and there was nothing to feel bad about. Nothing at all. Was there?

When the meeting broke up, as usual I put out the fire. Strangely enough, putting out the fire and leaving Stonehenge had become my favorite part of the meetings. I didn't know why. No, actually I sort of *did* know why.

Today Randall had gone off with everyone else, leaving Cheryl and me alone. Cheryl always waited for me. I liked that.

"You had me scared for a while," she said as I doused the fire. "I thought you were gonna say something that would break up the club."

"I wouldn't do that," I said, smiling. "It's too much fun."

"Sure is!" said Cheryl. I took her hand as we left Stonehenge. "So what was bothering you before?"

"I guess I started to feel bad about things."

"Never feel sorry for the enemy!" she said. "Does Austin feel bad every time he calls you the Gopher?"

"No, but I'm not talking about Austin. I feel sorry for Tyson."

"The slimeball? Why? All he ever does is say nasty things to people and fight. I don't feel sorry for him, and I don't trust him. We'll be lucky if the creep doesn't snitch on us."

"He won't snitch on us," I said.

"How can you be sure?"

"Because I am."

Then Cheryl stopped walking and a wide smile appeared on her face. "You did something, didn't you? You found a way to keep his mouth shut!"

"You could say that."

"What did you do?"

"I found out a secret. That's all."

Cheryl's ears seemed to pop up like a rabbit's. "Secret! You know a secret about Tyson McGaw? Tell me, tell me, I have to know!"

"No. I can't."

"Why not? I won't tell anyone."

"I have a deal with Tyson. I won't tell if he doesn't."

"I don't count, though," she begged.

"A deal's a deal."

"Who's gonna know?"

"I will."

"So Tyson's a better friend than I am?"

"No. Forget I said it. I don't want to talk about Tyson anymore."

Cheryl could see she was not going to get anywhere. She sighed. "Fine, *be* that way. I guess we'd better be getting back."

I didn't feel like going back though. It was warm for October, and it was just getting toward my favorite time of day.

"Wait a second, the road's that way," said Cheryl, pointing.

"No, it's not," I said playfully. "It's this way." I knew I was walking in the wrong direction, but I wanted to see if Cheryl would follow. She did. I ran in front of her.

"Jared, I think there's a cliff that way, be careful."

"C'mon," I said.

I slowed down as I heard the crash of waves somewhere far below. I could see the horizon through the trees, and soon I came out onto a grassy cliff above the ocean. Cheryl found me a moment later.

"See, I was right, bozo," she said. "I have a good sense of direction. You should have listened to me."

"I know," I said, with a silly smile on my face.

"C'mon, we'll be late!"

"I know," I said, with that same smile.

She looked at me, not quite sure what to make of it. "You're nuts, you know that?"

"I know," I said, and she laughed. Although I had come to Stonehenge in the worst of moods, I was in a good mood now, and I wanted that good mood to last. I was with my best friend and was having a great time.

"If my parents scream at me for missing supper, I'm blaming you," she said.

I smiled at that, and she smiled back. We sat down together close to the edge of the cliff, but not close enough to fall.

"We really *are* presidents of the club, aren't we?" I said.

"Yeah, we are."

"There's so much power in that, you know; being in charge of a club . . . I mean . . . five other kids letting us make decisions."

"Isn't it fun?" She squeezed my hand tightly.

"I think I like that the most—even more than I liked getting back at Austin. I like the power. It's like . . . it's like being king of a very small country. I think I'll run for class president this year."

Cheryl laughed.

"Why are you laughing at me?"

"I'm not laughing at you, I just think it'll be funny, because you'll be running against me."

"You're going to run for class president?"

"Sure, why not? Don't you think I'd be a good president?"

I smiled. "Yeah, I do."

"Hey, maybe we could run together—we're a team, right?" She looked at me, then we both looked out over the ocean, sort of afraid to look at each other for too long.

"The last time we got to talk alone like this was when we were up in the tree house," she said, "talking about how much we hate Austin and Rebecca."

"I don't want to talk about them," I said.

"Good. Then let's talk about Tyson's secret."

"I don't want to talk about that, either."

"Then what do you want to talk about?"

"Nothing, I guess."

I smiled, she smiled, and then, for no particular reason, I leaned over and I kissed her on the cheek. She instantly looked away from me.

I felt so stupid. I mean, here she was, my best friend, and I kissed her. How stupid could I get? My face turned as red as the sunset. I was going to say, "I'm sorry," but didn't have the guts to say much of anything at all.

Then she turned to me again and kissed me on the lips. Let me tell you, I didn't know how to feel just then. I felt so good about it, but at the same time, it felt so strange, as if we were doing something wrong. As if I wasn't supposed to be enjoying this. As if we wouldn't be friends anymore when the kiss ended.

But when the kiss ended, we were still friends—only our friendship was a little bit different, and I knew it would probably never be the old way again.

"Oh, boy . . . ," I said.

"Yeah . . . ," she said.

"Hmmm . . . ," I said.

"Well," I said. "What now?"

"I don't know."

"Nobody's going to believe us," I said.

"What do you mean?"

"No one ever believed us when we told them we were just friends, and we weren't going out. Now they'll never believe us."

"Are we going out now?"

"I don't know, are we?"

"I don't know, do you want to?"

"I don't know, do you?"

"I don't know," said Cheryl. "I always thought of you sort of like a brother."

"You thought of me like Randall?"

"Yuk! No way!"

"Well, then I guess you didn't think of me like a brother."

I tempted fate and kissed her again. Now I didn't care what anybody thought. I didn't care if people thought we were always going out. I didn't care if people said things. I didn't care if some golden rule was written across the sky saying that you can't go out with your best friend. I didn't care. Those were tree-house rules for tree-house friends, and the tree house had grown much too small these past few years.

Someone's Idea of a Joke

E **VERYTHING CHANGED** just a little bit after that
Friday afternoon. I found myself thinking a lot more
about Cheryl, and spending all my free time with her. Randall made a big deal about it, and tried to spread whatever
nasty rumors a kid brother can get away with spreading, but
it didn't bother us; we were having too good a time together
to worry about it. After a few days it was hard to imagine
what it was like before we started going out.

We knew this was just the start of a wonderful time in
both of our lives, and the next few months were going to be
great. I had a feeling that everything would start going my
way. In just a few weeks Coach Shuler would be choosing
the one runner to represent the school in the District
Olympics, and now I really believed that I would, just once,
beat out Austin. Between Cheryl, the Shadow Club, and the
progress I was making on the track team, I figured I had it
made.

Things never turn out the way you plan, though. Bad

things have a way of coming back at you, kind of like a boomerang. I don't think anyone ever gets away with any-thing, you know? Sure, maybe they think they might get away with things, but in the end—could be years later even—boom! That boomerang comes flying right back in their face.

The Shadow Club had a boomerang, and it seemed to pick up speed on its way back. It was a strange boomerang that nobody quite expected and nobody quite understood, but it hit every single one of us so quickly, so furiously, that we never knew what hit us.

There are lots of good jokes you could pull on somebody's locker. You could hide in it, and scare the daylights out of them when they opened it. You could put a rotten egg in it; that's always good for a laugh. You could set up a bucket of water that would pour on their head when they opened it; that was always good for a laugh, too.

But what Eric Kilfoil, the star basketball player, found when he opened his locker was not funny at all. It was no joke; it was downright nasty. Everything was there, just where he had left it before basketball practice, but things were definitely not the same. Someone had gone into his locker and drenched everything, his clothes, his new sweats, even his books, with black paint. And not the kind that comes out, either. This was thick stuff that could never wash out. He was so mad, he began to kick all the lockers. I could hear it all the way out on the track.

His clothes were ruined, his books were ruined, even his science project was ruined, and you know what?

The Shadow Club *didn't do it!*

There are tricks and there are tricks. This was just plain mean, and Darren, who saw the locker, had no idea who would do such a thing, or why.

Eric Kilfoil became the first mysterious victim in a wave of unexplained crimes.

There was a locker search next Monday. Everyone knows that locker searches are illegal, but that doesn't matter much when someone steals the principal's eight-hundred-dollar camera.

Mr. Diller, the principal, was the kind of guy who thought that the kids in our school were to blame for all of Earth's problems, and he was sure one of us must have stolen his camera. He had us all line up by our lockers, one class at a time, and one by one he searched each locker, leaving no stone unturned. You see, that camera was his life, and any kid caught with it was going to see trouble like no one had ever seen before. I'd never seen Diller this mad. Ralphy Sherman said that he had seen a bum walking away with it, which just made Diller more certain it was still in school.

My row of lockers was the last one to be checked.

One by one Mr. Diller had us open our lockers, to prove to him we didn't have his camera, and one by one we cleared ourselves of blame.

Then he came to Tommy Nickols, O.P.'s archenemy. Tommy opened his locker, just like the rest of us. It was a mess: papers everywhere, old library books that were way overdue, and a black strap sticking out from beneath them. Tommy looked up at Diller, then back down at his locker, and Diller reached in, pulling on the strap. Out came his eight-hundred-dollar camera.

"I didn't do it!" was all Tommy could say. "It wasn't me, it wasn't me!" But the evidence was staring us all in the face.

Tommy began to cry, even harder than he did when Octavia got stomped on. "I didn't do it!" he wailed, over and over again.

I looked across at O.P., Cheryl, and Darren. I could tell by the looks on their faces that they had nothing to do with this. This was not a Shadow Club prank, and I believed Tommy Nickols. Tommy was a good kid, and this stank of sabotage. Someone had planted that camera, I knew it, but I couldn't figure out who would do such a thing.

Mr. Diller, on the other hand, believed what he saw. Tommy Nickols, the ninth grade's best student, was suspended for three days.

David Berger, in spite of the sliming event, was still chosen to play a solo with the high school band, and as usual, he made everyone in the junior high band feel lousy about it.

One afternoon, as the buses were loading up to go home, David came running out of his bus like a maniac. It was just before track practice, and I was talking with Cheryl—which I was doing quite a lot of lately—when he came bursting between us and asked, "Hey, has anybody seen my trumpet?"

"Why would we have seen your trumpet?" answered Cheryl.

He ran to another group of kids, desperately asking, "Has anybody seen my trumpet? I think it's been stolen!"

He asked every kid who came out of school, ran into the school, then came out a few minutes later. He was near tears. "I checked all the classrooms. I know I had it with me. Somebody stole it!"

None of us thought much of it until about thirty seconds later, when the buses began to pull out, and a horrible crunching noise sounded from the back tires of bus number five.

When David saw it, he nearly dove beneath the wheels to save his trumpet, but it was too late. By the time the bus driver realized what was going on and stopped the bus, David Berger's silver trumpet had been crushed flat, never to play, or slime anyone ever again. He held it up and tried to push down on one of the valves, but it didn't move. He tried a bit harder, and the valve fell off; the thing might as well have been flattened by a steamroller. David sort of wandered off in shock, holding his trumpet as if it were a baby.

A minute later, Jason Perez ran up to Cheryl and me.

"I didn't do it," he said. "I didn't, honestly, I didn't!" and I knew he was telling the truth. It seemed that someone else had picked up the pranks where we had left off. It was as if all the hatred built up by the Shadow Club became an invisible monster that went around pulling its own horrible pranks. I knew there had to be a more logical explanation, though.

"Well, maybe all these kids have other enemies, too," said Cheryl. "Maybe it's all just coincidence."

"Maybe," I said, "or maybe someone's trying to frame us."

Greene's Eye

T ELL ME ABOUT the Shadow Club, Jared."

Mr. Greene sat in his tiny office, with the venetian blinds open. I could barely see his face, because the sky behind him was so bright. All I could see was his silhouette. My heart seemed to stop for at least five seconds when he asked me the question.

"The Shadow Club? What's that?" I said. It was a stupid thing to say, but he had caught me off guard.

"Something you know about," said Mr. Greene. I had gotten a note during third period that said he wanted to see me during lunch. It didn't take me long to figure out that Tyson had told him about the club.

"Oh, oh that," I said. This wasn't going to be easy. "It's just a group of kids. We get together, go to the movies, play board games, you know."

"Why do you call it the Shadow Club?" he asked, twiddling his thumbs and sitting in his big chair, behind his big desk, in that small room.

"Because we meet late in the afternoon," I said. "When there's lots of shadows. Can I go now?"

"Not yet. I'd like to know a little more about the club first."

"Like what?"

"Like who's in it."

"Is it all right if I eat my lunch in here?" I asked. He nodded. I began to chow down my sandwich, and shut up real quick. I ate my sandwich, my chips, and Greene waited until I was down to the core of my apple before he spoke again.

"You never answered my question."

"Which one?"

"Who's in the Shadow Club?"

"Me!" I said, smiling.

"Who else?" asked Greene.

"Hard to remember. Like I said, there's lots of shadows. I don't see their faces. Can I go now?"

"No, not yet."

I sighed and looked at my wrist, pretending I had a watch. Be calm, I thought to myself. Don't sweat. If I sweat, he'll know I'm scared. I couldn't let him know that. I looked up at him, but all I could see was the dark blob of his big head.

"Could you close the blinds?" I asked. "The sun's in my eyes."

"Certainly." He turned around, and shut the blinds. Now I could see his face; his eyes watched me from behind those

thick glasses. I decided that I liked it better when I couldn't
see him.

"Why won't you tell me who's in the club, Jared?" he
asked.

I sighed. "Because it's a secret club," I said. "I'm sworn to
secrecy."

Greene didn't seem to react at all. He just sat there,
staring out at me from behind his bug-eyed glasses. "Secret
club?"

"Yeah, weren't you ever in a secret club when you were a
kid? Is there something wrong with that?"

"I don't know," he said. "That's what I want to find out."

I stood up. It was very intimidating, the way Greene sat
there staring at me, and it was so hard not to tell him everything he wanted to know. But if I did, I knew he would put
two and two together. He would figure out about all the
tricks we did—and worse, we would end up getting the
blame for David's trumpet, and the other nasty tricks that we
had nothing to do with. I couldn't tell him a thing. I began
to pace around the room, looking at things: the books on his
shelf, a diploma on the wall, a filing cabinet with a lock on
it. This office made me nervous. I felt like I was in jail, getting the third degree.

"Who told you about the club, anyway?" I asked, knowing full well who did.

"It doesn't matter," he said.

"It was Tyson McGaw, wasn't it?"

Then Greene leaned forward and took off his glasses. Without his glasses, his eyes seemed a lot smaller. "Leave Tyson out of this."

"I'll bet it was him!"

"Give Tyson a break," said Greene. "He's got enough problems without you making things worse, believe me."

"What kind of problems?" I asked, sitting down again.

Greene waited for a while, as if he was going to tell me something, but instead he said, "It doesn't matter." He thought for a moment, then said, "You know, Tyson thinks an awful lot of you."

I looked away from Greene's small eyes. He looked funny without glasses. He looked more like a person, and less like a vice principal.

"Why?" I asked.

"I don't know. I guess because you're a good kid." He smiled. That made me feel a little uncomfortable. I don't know why. That cold feeling in my hands came back, along with that sick feeling I had at our last meeting at Stonehenge.

"I barely even know him," I said.

"Why don't you get to know him?"

I shrugged. "I have my own friends. I have the track team. I don't have time for that."

"I see." Mr. Greene nodded, and looked at me for a long time, as vice principals like to do, and then he asked, "Is the Shadow Club a gang, Jared?"

I couldn't believe he actually thought that! I just sat there, dumbfounded.

"You know, we've never had trouble with gangs here."

"The Shadow Club isn't a gang!" I said.

"How can I believe that?"

"You have to believe it! It's just a bunch of good kids having a good time, that's all."

"All by yourselves, without any adult supervision?"

"Exactly."

"I don't like the sound of that."

By now that little room he called his office felt like a cage. I sunk deeper into the hard wood chair, figuring Greene would just keep picking on the club. He didn't. Instead he started talking about something else I didn't want to think about.

"Aren't the District Olympics coming up, Jared?" he asked.

"Yeah, in about a month." I squirmed in my seat, trying to get comfortable. There was no way to get comfortable in that chair.

"I hear you could be running for our school," he said.

"Me or Austin Pace. It depends on who has a faster time," I said through clenched teeth, because I knew Austin's time was still better than mine.

Mr. Greene nodded. "You know, Jared, I'd hate to see you disqualified because you've done something stupid."

"What do you mean?" I asked.

"I mean that if this 'club' of yours gets you into trouble, you could be suspended from the team."

"Mr. Greene," I said, "our club has nothing to do with school—we don't even meet at school. Can't you just leave us alone?"

"It's my job to make sure our kids don't get into trouble!"

"C'mon, Mr. Greene, what kind of trouble could kids like us get into?"

"Kids like who?"

"Like me, and Cheryl, and Jason Perez, and O.P. Han, and . . ." I stopped as soon as I realized what I was doing. He'd tricked me! He'd tricked me into leaking out information about the club! If I said one word too many, I could have been signing the Shadow Club's death warrant.

"Jason and O.P. are in this club?"

I didn't say a word.

Greene leaned back in his chair, and rocked a bit, like he had the whole world in the palms of his hands. Until that day, I sort of liked Mr. Greene; of course he never talked to me much, but he seemed like a nice guy. Now, sitting there at that desk, he seemed mean. He seemed nasty. He seemed like the one person who could destroy the Shadow Club just because we were having a good time. I suddenly realized that I hated Mr. Greene. I wished he had never been born.

"I'll tell you what, Jared," he said, "you don't have to tell me anything else about your club. You've never gotten into trouble before, and your teachers always have good things to say about you, so I'll trust you . . . but there's one condition."

"What?"

Mr. Greene leaned a bit closer. "I want you to let Tyson join your club."

I backed away as if I had been slapped in the face. "No!" I said straight out. "No way! He can't!"

"Jared, I'm asking you a favor. It would mean a lot to him."

"You don't understand," I said. "He can't because . . ."

"Because what?"

"Because he can't!" I said. "It's a special club, and only certain kids are allowed in it!"

"I can't accept that. If your club is just a social club, like you say it is, then you can let Tyson in. Or is there something about your club you'd rather I didn't know?"

"No!"

"Then let Tyson join."

"No!"

"But, Jared . . ."

"No! No! No!" I said. "No!" Period. The end. "No!"

I stood up, and nearly smashed my fist on the desk, I was so angry. Mr. Greene, on the other hand, couldn't have been calmer. He just leaned back in his chair, twiddling his thumbs again. He stared at me for a long time, like vice principals do. This time, I didn't look back at him.

"Can I go now?" I asked.

"Close the door on your way out, Jared" was all he said.

I stood there for a moment longer, but he didn't say anything else, so I turned and went to the door. Just as my hand touched the doorknob I heard him speak.

"Answer me one question, Jared," he said. I didn't look at him; I kept my eyes fixed on the doorknob. "Has the Shadow Club done anything wrong?"

I still looked down at the doorknob. "No," I said.

"OK, fine . . . but I want you to know, Jared, that I'm keeping my eye on you. I don't like this club of yours; there's something about it that smells. I'm going to be watching you like a hawk, and if you're lying to me, Jared, you'll be in a lot of trouble."

I left, closing the door behind me as quickly as I could, and ran down the hall to get far, far away from that horrible little man in his horrible little office.

What Ralphy Said

WHEN THINGS GET bad, boy, do they get bad. I thought that maybe—*maybe*—if the Shadow Club laid low for a while and didn't play any tricks, then Greene might leave us alone; maybe everything would be all right. But things weren't all right.

I had hoped that David Berger's flattened trumpet would be the last of the mysterious pranks, but it was not. Someone was terrorizing the unbeatables; someone who didn't care how much the unbeatables got hurt, or how much property was destroyed, and this person, whoever it was, thought they could get away with it by blaming the Shadow Club. There was only one person who knew enough about the Shadow Club to do that: Tyson McGaw.

"I say we give him what he deserves," said Randall, as we sat around Stonehenge at our next meeting.

"Yeah," said Darren. "We should beat the daylights out of him, and force him to confess!"

"And then get him expelled from school for it," added Jason. Everyone else agreed.

"No!" I said. "We have no proof—we can't do anything like that yet."

"What other proof do we need?" asked Abbie. "He's the only other one who knows about the club. It has to be him!"

"We can't do anything yet, though," I said. "Not until we can prove he's doing the pranks."

"He's innocent until proven guilty," added Cheryl, "even though we know he's guilty."

"So what do we do?" asked O.P. "Sit around and wait to be blamed for everything? What if something *really* bad happens?"

"Don't worry," I said. "Tyson's crazy, but not *that* crazy. Nothing really bad is going to happen."

Boy, was I wrong.

That next week, the entire club vowed to look out for the unbeatables; watching them as well as watching Tyson, to make sure that no more pranks were pulled. We must have done a lousy job of it though, because on Thursday, during lunch, Drew Landers became the next victim.

Drew, as I've told you, is a swimmer, and very much into it; in fact, he had this obsession with anything that had to do with swimming. It only made sense, then, that Drew had a thing for fish. For as long as I knew Drew, he had always had a fish tank—it was the one thing in his room that he kept clean—and he had a second tank in school, in Mr. Milburn's room. I guess because he considered himself a human fish, he had a weird sort of affection for his "cousins" in the tank.

Anyway, that sixty-gallon tank had sat in Mr. Milburn's classroom since Drew started seventh grade, and now, a year later, it was still there, filled with starfish, sea anemones, and brightly colored saltwater fish. They were pretty, they were expensive, and Drew loved those fish like most normal people might love a pet dog.

Every once in a while, some bozo would drop something stupid into the tank: a bar of soap or maybe the shavings from the classroom pencil sharpener. Once, someone put red food coloring in the tank. After Mr. Milburn changed the water, the fish seemed fine, although they were sort of pink for a while. No matter what dumb things kids did to that tank, those fish always seemed to come out of their ordeals all right. But not this time.

During lunch Mr. Milburn always locked his room and went down to the teachers' lounge to fall asleep while listening to the rest of the teachers gossip. Well, as everyone knows, school classroom locks are the easiest in the world to pick; all you have to do is slide a hanger into the doorjamb and bingo!

Well, that's what someone did, and then that same someone dropped a firecracker into Drew's fish tank.

Now, there are firecrackers and there are *firecrackers*. There are the kind they call "safe and sane," and there are the kind that are more like hand grenades. There are cherry bombs and M-80's that, when put in a strategic location, can do an awful lot of damage, but the worst by far are blockbusters. Packed into the cylinder of a blockbuster is a quarter stick of dynamite, and when one goes off, it can be heard for miles.

I don't know how they did it, but someone rigged up a blockbuster to go off in that fish tank, and when it blew, nothing in the room was safe. The tank turned into one huge bomb, sending glass and water flying in all directions, shredding plants and tearing paper on the walls. The room became a war zone.

I was out on the field with Cheryl and Randall, consoling Randall from his recent humiliation. It seemed that the day before, after swim practice, Drew threw Randall out of the locker room with no clothes on. Almost the second I had convinced Randall it was better to forget about it for a while, we heard the explosion. BOOM! It was so loud you'd swear the whole school had blown up. The blast echoed from the high school, across the large field, and a strange silence followed. Everyone turned toward the school.

"Not again," said Cheryl. At first we all thought this was yet another school fire, but in a moment I began to suspect it was another evil prank. I turned to look for Tyson but couldn't find him, and that sick feeling returned to my stomach, along with the cold feeling to my hands. Meanwhile, several teachers ran into the school to evacuate the remaining students; for all they knew, a gas line could have blown up. Someone pulled the fire alarm, and in minutes the fire trucks arrived. It didn't take long for the firemen to find out what had happened.

From what I heard, there was nothing left of the fish tank, and that collection of fish that Drew Landers had spent years putting together was gone in a fiery fraction of a second.

"Tell me the truth, Randall," said a kid after school. Cheryl and I were talking before I went off to track practice, and, as usual, Randall was hanging around with us, making obnoxious comments about the fact that we spent so much time together, when this kid—someone on the swim team, I guess—came up to us and asked Randall a question.

"Tell me the truth," he asked. "Did you blow up Drew's fish tank? Tell me the truth, I won't tell anyone."

Randall was speechless. He turned to Cheryl. "See? See, what did I tell you? Just because of what he did to me yesterday, everyone's gonna think that I blew up his tank! I'm being framed!" he yelled, then he turned to the kid. "No! I didn't do it, so just get out of here, all right?"

"Yeah, I'll *bet* you didn't do it!" said the kid, and ran off.

"You better keep your mouth shut, because I didn't!" yelled Randall, as the kid ran away. He turned to me and

Cheryl. "You know I didn't, right? I was there with you all during lunch, you know I was."

"I know, and you know, but who's going to believe us?" I said.

"I see a pattern emerging," said Cheryl. "Have you noticed that these pranks have been pulled soon after the victim has done something really mean to a member of the Shadow Club?"

"Huh?" said Randall.

"Think about it, blimp brain," said Cheryl to her brother. "Eric Kilfoil's locker was filled with paint the day after Darren nearly got into a fight with him—Darren told me about that. David Berger's trumpet got run over the day after David was chosen to play for the high school band again, and he'd made Jason feel miserable about it. Tommy Nickols had just beat out O.P. for a place in the district science fair before the camera incident, and now Drew's fish tank explodes the day after he threw you out of the locker room naked!"

"Then someone is definitely trying to frame us!"

"Exactly," said Cheryl. "And if anyone finds out about the club, then we're going to be the prime suspects—we're the only ones with motives!"

"We're already suspects," I said, "because someone already knows about the club." Cheryl and Randall turned to me with that end-of-the-world look in their eyes. "Greene knows. I don't think he knows what we've done, but he knows about the club, and I'm sure he suspects us." Until then, I hadn't told anyone.

"How?" asked Cheryl.

"Tyson told him. I'm sure of it."

"Tyson!" said Randall, with a hiss in his voice that made him sound like a snake. "I told you he was behind all this."

"It has to be!" said Cheryl.

"I'll bet we could prove Tyson blew up the fish tank!" said Randall. "Fingerprints or something."

And then another voice entered the conversation. "I saw him do it," said the voice. We all turned around, and standing there, braces, freckles, curly hair, and all, was Ralphy Sherman.

"You're talking about the fish tank, right?" said Ralphy. "Well, I saw Tyson McGaw blow it up."

We were all quiet. Ralphy blew a big fat bubble-gum bubble, and it popped in his face, sticking to his eyebrows. He peeled it off and popped it back into his mouth.

"It's true," he said. "I was in the classroom. I saw."

"How could you have been in the classroom? You would have been killed by the exploding tank," Cheryl said.

"Well, not *in* the classroom, but looking in through the window. I saw Tyson do it. Honest."

"But I saw you in the field when it went off, Ralphy," said Randall.

"Darn right," said Ralphy. "I wasn't going to hang around if a blockbuster's about to go off. I left as quickly as I could."

We all looked at Ralphy—Ralphy Sherman who couldn't pass a true-or-false exam because he didn't know the difference. Should we believe this? Ralphy blew another bubble, this one bigger than his whole head, and when it popped it stuck to his hair. He peeled it away and shoved the gum back into his mouth.

"You know what?" I said. "I believe him!"

"Me, too," said Cheryl.

"So do I," said Randall.

Ralphy's eyes lit up. "You do? Really, honestly, truly, you believe me?"

"Yeah," I said.

Ralphy smiled, and skipped off toward his bus, the happiest boy in the world.

We didn't get a moment's rest that day, for only thirty seconds after Ralphy went skipping away, we turned to see a commotion at the school's front gate.

"Hey," yelled Martin Bricker, to anyone who would listen. "Vera can't stop her bike, and she's headed toward Sellar Boulevard!"

Cheryl, Randall, and I raced toward the front gate, but it was too late. As we looked down the street, we could see Vera flying down the hill, screaming at the top of her lungs.

Of course, I thought to myself. What an idiot I was! Didn't Abbie have a big argument with Vera today? Didn't Vera call her a slob in front of half the grade, or something

like that? Of course Vera would be the next victim, if Tyson
were trying to frame the club.

We watched in horror as she crossed through the first intersection on the way to Sellar Boulevard, which was down
at the bottom of the hill. Luckily it was a small intersection,
and no cars were there at the time. But Sellar Boulevard
would be a different story; it was one of the busiest streets in
town and I could see cars and buses racing across it.

"She's gonna get herself killed!" yelled someone from the
crowd, as we all watched Vera fly down the street. "Can't
somebody stop her?" If she had half a brain she would have
turned and smashed into a fence rather than race across Sellar Boulevard, but as anyone could tell you, Vera Donaldson
did not have half a brain.

In seconds she came up on Sellar Boulevard and went
flying out into the middle of traffic. Car horns blared, a van
swerved, a car screeched to a halt and was rear-ended.

Vera sailed across the street, hit the curb, and went
bouncing off of her bike, hitting her head on a fire hydrant,
while the bike went crashing through Muggleson's Bakery
window, laying the window to waste and demolishing a five-
layer wedding cake on display.

Everyone, including Cheryl and Randall, ran down the
street to find out how Vera was, but I didn't. There was
someone who I had to find, and I had to find him now.

It didn't take long. He was standing by his locker in the
main hallway.

"Tyson . . . ," I snarled, "you're gonna pay for this!"

"Get out of my face," he grunted and tried to leave, but I grabbed him by his shirt, and as he struggled, I dragged him through the hall.

"Leave me alone, you moron! You idiot! You butt head!"

I didn't say anything. Not yet. Not until I had him in a place where no one would hear us.

I dragged him down the hall, and shoved him in the school phone booth, closing the door behind us. He struggled, and I shook him so hard that he began to look like one of those marionettes he had up on his wall.

"Listen up, and listen good," I said. "I know what you've been doing, and you're not going to get away with it."

"I don't know what you're talking about!" he screamed. I put my hand over his mouth so he couldn't scream. He bit it, and I pushed him back so hard that the telephone receiver went flying off the hook. I could hear the dial tone.

"If you scream one more time, slimeball, I'm gonna hit you so hard your next of kin will feel it, too!" That shut him up. "I said, I know what you've been doing. I know you're trying to frame us, and I think it really stinks. I think *you* stink, slimeball, and I'm telling you right now that if there's one more prank, if another 'unbeatable' gets hurt, you're gonna have all seven of us in the club coming down on you so hard you won't know what hit you!"

"I don't know what you're talking about!" he screamed.

"Shut up! You know exactly what I'm talking about. You told Greene about our club, and now you're trying to get us all in trouble. Why did you tell Greene, anyway? Couldn't you have left well enough alone?"

"All right!" he said. "I admit I told Greene, but I didn't do anything else!"

"Liar!" I said.

"And I didn't do it to be mean! Now leave me alone!"

"Then why did you tell him?"

He didn't answer me.

"WHY DID YOU TELL HIM?" I pushed him. The door to the phone booth flew open, and Tyson flew out, falling to the ground. "Why did you tell him?" I screamed. He didn't answer. He got up and ran down the hall as quickly as he could. I watched him run, brimming with anger. I couldn't remember having ever hated anyone as much; not even Austin.

Then I began to yell, hoping everyone left in school heard me.

"Bed wetter!" I yelled. "Bed wetter! Tyson pees in his bed!" It echoed through the halls and the sound lingered long after Tyson had burst through the school's front doors.

I shouldn't have gone to track practice that day. I should have just run home and buried myself in my homework—or better yet, buried myself in my pillow and hidden like an ostrich until this whole thing passed over. That's what I should have done, but I didn't. Instead, I ran out to the field to be with the track team, and that was a mistake, because, as everyone knows, bad luck comes in threes. First on that fateful day came the fish tank, then Vera's bike, and then came the nastiest run-in I ever had with Austin Pace.

By the time I arrived at practice, Austin was leading the stretching exercises, and Coach Shuler was nowhere to be seen. I was about ten minutes late, and it was never good to be late for practice.

"Well, lookie here," said Austin. "The Gopher finally decided to show up!"

"Hi, Gopher," said Martin Bricker. Kids didn't even say it to be mean anymore. They just said it like it was my name.

"Give me twenty push-ups for being late, Gopher." I dropped and gave him twenty. When I was done, Austin had the whole team sit down, as he opened a large carton that was on the ground.

"Here are our team uniforms," he said. Everyone was pleased to hear that, and for a few minutes I was glad I had decided to go to practice that day. "Coach Shuler will be out in a minute with the team sweats."

Austin opened the box, and began to hand them out. "Miller," he said, tossing Greg Miller his top and matching shorts. This was the first year that the team actually got new sweats and uniforms that had each kid's name on them. Some said it was because the track team deserved it, but most knew it was because Austin's father had made a big donation to the team.

"Bricker!" yelled Austin, as he tossed Martin's shirt and shorts to him. I waited patiently, and he finally got around to mine.

"Mercer," he said, throwing me my uniform. It felt good to hold the brand-new uniform of the team; that smooth feel of the light, colorful material, and that new smell it had. It reminded me that our first meet was coming up soon, and I could hardly wait! My times were getting better, and although they weren't quite as fast as Austin's, they were pretty good. Now, to make it complete, I had a uniform with my name on it. I felt like a real runner, and for a minute it made me forget about my other troubles.

I couldn't wait to try on the shirt, so although it was a bit chilly, I took off my shirt and was about to try the new one on, when I caught a glimpse of the bright red name written across the back.

It said GOPHER.

I sat there for a few moments, letting it sink in. Gopher. My team shirt said Gopher.

"Austin," I said. "This better not be mine." I threw it back at his face, waiting to see what he would say. He caught it, and looked at it.

"Nope. Gopher. That's you." He threw it back at me. I clenched my hands into fists, and gritted my teeth.

"It says Gopher?" asked one of the seventh graders. "Let me see, let me see!" He grabbed it, and I grabbed it back.

"My name is Mercer, not Gopher!" I threw the shirt at Austin's face again. He caught it.

"Didn't you want Gopher on your shirt? That's how everyone knows you." He threw it back in my face.

"No!" I said. I would never wear it. Never.

"Well, it's too late," said Austin. "The shirts and sweats have already been made up."

"That's written on my sweats, too?"

"Of course."

That did it. I dropped the shirt, and lunged at him. How could he do that? Not only did *he* humiliate me, but he was trying to force me to humiliate myself by wearing that word on my shirt. I swung my fist, missing his face by less than an inch. I swung again, but by then a dozen hands were on me, holding me back. "Let go of me!" I screamed, but the team just held me and wouldn't let me get a clear shot at Austin. I struggled and kicked but they wouldn't let me go.

"Look at him," somebody yelled. "He's fighting like Tyson fights!" That only made me struggle harder. Then, out of nowhere, Coach Shuler appeared and pulled me out of the hands of the others, shaking me so hard that my brain rattled.

"What do you think you're doing, Jared? Stop it! Stop it now!" My head hurt from the shake-up, and my arms went limp. "This is a team, Jared," he said, "and you had better remember that. You don't start fights with your team captain. I don't care what your differences are, you don't fight with him."

"But . . ."

"Did you hear me? I said that you don't fight with Austin. Is that clear?"

I stood there, catching my breath. I wouldn't give him as much as a nod. "He put 'Gopher' on my uniform!"

The coach turned to Austin, and Austin shrugged.

"Honest mistake," Austin said.

"We'll settle this after practice," said the coach. That's when Austin came up to me.

"Now, c'mon," said Austin, holding out his hand to shake. "Let's forget about this whole thing, all right?"

I looked at his hand. I have to admit, I almost did it. I thought about shaking Austin's hand and eating my pride for the sake of the team, but then he said, "C'mon, be a good gopher, and forget about it."

My hands clenched into fists again. I wouldn't shake his hand after that—I wouldn't even stand in the same field with him. I picked up my backpack, shoved my disgusting gopher shirt into it, and I walked. The coach tried to follow, so I ran. I ran to the edge of the field, and kept running, putting as much distance between me and Austin Pace as I could. A moment later I realized that someone was running with me.

"I saw the whole thing." It was Cheryl. "I think it was awful. Austin's a real creep."

Great! The last thing I wanted was for Cheryl to see Austin humiliate me.

"Jared," called the coach, "let's talk about this." But I ignored him.

"What are you doing here, anyway?" I asked her.

"I came to tell you that Vera is all right. She bumped her head, but she'll be all right."

It was good to hear, but it didn't make me feel any better. I ducked through a hole in the fence and into the woods. Cheryl followed. I kept running through the trees, getting scratches on my arms from branches, but still that anger wouldn't leave.

"Jared, slow down," said Cheryl. "I can't keep up with you!"

I stopped. We were far from the field now.

"You know what?" I said. "I hope Tyson was watching and gets Austin next. I hope Tyson pulls a terrible trick so mean that Austin never gets over it, that's what I hope!"

Cheryl looked at me kind of strange. "You really want that?" she asked.

I thought for a moment, catching my breath. "I don't

know what I want." It was true. I didn't know how I felt, or what I wanted. I didn't even know who to hate anymore: Austin, Tyson, the Shadow Club, or maybe just myself for allowing all this to happen.

"Hey," said Cheryl, taking my hand, "whadaya say you come over to my house and we make chocolate shakes like we used to?"

I put my normal shirt back on and reluctantly said, "OK."

She put her arms around my neck and kissed me. "Things'll be OK," she said. I wanted to believe it, so I kissed her again. Then, with my arm around her shoulder, we went off to her house.

Used to be, drinking a chocolate shake would make any problem disappear, but even as I sat there in Cheryl's living room, watching TV and filling up on chocolate shakes, I knew that it would take a whole lot more to solve these problems.

The Next Victim

MORNING CAME AFTER a lousy night of night-mares—dreams about my parents turning into go-phers, dreams about being stepped on by a sixty-foot-tall Austin Pace in huge white Aeropeds, dreams about being trapped in a fish tank that was about to explode. Nasty stuff. I woke up with a headache.

My parents could tell that something was bugging me, but when they asked what it was, I didn't tell them about the pranks and about Tyson. I simply told them, as I always did, that Austin Pace was the problem.

"Him again?" said my father, before he left for work. "Don't worry about him. Austin Paces are a dime a dozen, but there's only one Jared Mercer." He smiled and mussed up my hair with his hand, which I used to like, before I discov-ered the importance of the hairbrush.

"Don't let him get to you," said my mom, which was easy to say, but hard to live by.

"Dad . . . ," I said, as he was about to leave. For a split

second I felt like telling both of them everything about the Shadow Club, what we did, how we were being framed—everything—but no. What kind of club president would I be if I told my parents?

"Forget it," I said. "See you tonight."

My father left, and I went off to school. If I could have told them, it could have ended right there, but I guess I just didn't have sense enough to do that. I had to get sense knocked into me the hard way.

As I crossed the field on my way to school that Friday morning, I saw Austin running his morning laps in his Aeropeds, as he did every stupid little morning of his stupid little life. I wouldn't look at him. I looked up, I looked down, I looked at the grass, the sky, the bleachers—anything but Austin. And because I was so intent on not looking at him, I ended up tripping over some sharp, jagged rocks sticking out of the ground in the middle of the field.

Wonderful, I thought. *Now* Austin will laugh at me for tripping over my own feet. He didn't, though. He kept on running and ignored me. I got off the field as fast as I could without making it look like I was hurrying.

As I entered the school, it began to hit me that there were only two unbeatables left to be hit by Tyson: Austin and Rebecca. That's when Cheryl came up to me.

"There you are," she said. "I've been looking all over for

you." She looked at my hands. "What happened to *you?*" she asked.

I looked at them. They were scratched up a bit from when I had fallen in the field. "I tripped. That's all."

"I've been on Tyson patrol," she said. "I think the whole club should take shifts watching him."

"Where is he?"

"I haven't seen him yet," she said.

That's when something clicked inside my head. Something dark and scary began to come into clear focus. It began slowly. First I looked at my hands again, at the scratches. Those rocks I had tripped over weren't there the day before; they couldn't have been. What were such sharp rocks doing buried in the middle of the field anyway? The middle of the field! Oh no! Oh no! *No!*

Cheryl must have seen it in my eyes. "What's the matter?" she asked.

"Austin!" I yelled. "We have to stop Austin!" I turned and ran, sprinting down the hall, knocking down kids and teachers, running at my top speed to the exit. Far behind me I could hear Cheryl calling my name, but I didn't have time to stop. I may have already been too late.

I burst through the double doors, knocking down two kids. "Austin!" I screamed as I ran, for as well as I knew that those rocks hadn't been there the day before, I also knew that Austin sprinted across the center of the oval field once every single day—BAREFOOT! Everyone knew he did it, but I was the only one who knew about the rocks; only I could stop him!

I ran out from between the bleachers in time to see Austin race across the grass, barefoot, leaving his Aeropeds far behind as he headed toward the rocks. Of all of the mixed-up feelings inside of me, one thing was certain; I wanted with all my heart to stop Austin from running through that minefield of razor-sharp stones!

"Austin!" I screamed. "Austin, stop!" but he wouldn't; he would never stop in the middle of a race. I ran through the grass to try to catch him, but I wasn't fast enough, I just wasn't fast enough! All I could do was watch as he hit the rocks.

First his left foot fell onto them, and it broke his perfect stride. He tried to keep his balance, and that's when his right foot came down on them. He slid, and then an instant later he was flying through the air, forced head over heels by the tremendous speed of his own body.

I went to him and almost had to turn away from what I saw. It was horrible. Austin had hit the worst of the rocks in the worst of ways. The soles of both his feet had been gashed open, and his left foot seemed twisted in a nasty position.

Austin saw them and began to scream. "No! No! My feet!" He yelled, "My feet, my feet, my feet!" over and over again. I could see the pain was just beginning to set in. I knelt before him. There was blood everywhere, and I didn't know what to do.

"My feet, my feet! No! Not my feet! Anything but my feet!"

I took off my shirt and pressed it against one foot, to hold back the bleeding, and he yelled, "Ow! My ankle! It's broken! My ankle's broken! My ankle! My ankle!"

I didn't know much about broken ankles, but something definitely did look wrong. His foot was twisted real funny, and whenever I tried to move it he shrieked. It was beginning to puff up and turn blue.

"No! Not my feet!" he cried.

My shirt began to turn red.

"It's all right," I said, even though I knew it wasn't all right. "You'll be fine."

Then he looked at me, and I'm pretty sure that was the first time he realized it was me helping him.

"Gopher!" he said. "My feet . . . My feet!"

By now other kids began to gather around, and teachers were running out from the school.

"Give me a shirt," I demanded, and three kids tossed me their shirts. I pressed one of them to Austin's other foot.

"My feet," he mumbled, through his tears.

"You'll be all right."

"No! No, you don't understand!" he cried. "My father wants me to go to the Olympics. I have to go. He's counting on me. I have to. I have to run." Austin's face was getting redder and redder from his tears. "I've been training for years. Years! Next year I'm getting a private coach. My feet! I can't run if my feet are . . ." He looked down at them. "No! What will I do? What will I do? What will I tell my father? He'll kill me! My ankle! It hurts! He'll kill me! What will I do?" Austin broke down and just cried like a baby, until it almost made me cry.

In a moment, Mr. Diller, our principal, came and carried Austin to the nurse's office. I was about to follow, but first I ran to the tip of the oval, picked up Austin's Aeropeds, and brought them along.

Whatever Austin had done to me in the past, whatever humiliation he had ever rubbed my nose in, he didn't deserve this. He was Olympics-bound; running was his life. It wasn't my life. For me running was something I could do that I liked doing, but for Austin, it was even more important. His feet would need stitches, but worse than that, his ankle would take months to heal. Who knew how long it would be till he could run again, if ever.

Sure, now I was fastest on the team, but all at once I didn't care anymore. Believe it or not, I cared more about Austin's feet.

I followed Austin and Mr. Diller to the nurse's office and watched as they tended to Austin's feet, until they shut the door. Still, I could hear his sobs. I stood there for at least five minutes, without realizing I had no shirt on. My shirt was ruined now, but there was another shirt in my backpack; my track team gopher shirt. I put it on, and sat outside the door. Soon Cheryl showed up, and the nurse suggested that I go to class, but I refused. I let Cheryl go, and I waited.

Finally the nurse let me in the office to keep Austin company while she called his parents. Inside, it smelled like alcohol and blood. Austin's feet were all wrapped up now; the white gauze was the same color as his Aeropeds. They had splinted the broken one. I still held his Aeropeds, and I placed them on the chair next to him.

"Thanks for helping me, Jared," he said, his eyes still a bit wet. I smiled. It was the first time he'd called me Jared all year.

"It's OK," I said. "I'm sorry about what happened."

He swallowed. "I guess I've been a real snot to you," he said.

"Yeah," I admitted. "It's OK, though."

"I guess it's because I'm real competitive, you know. My father says it's good to be competitive. I don't know. I guess all these years you were the only one who came close to being as fast as me. It scared me. It was like if one person could come close to beating me, then I wasn't good enough for the Olympics."

He looked at me, and I just listened.

"I guess . . . I guess we could have been real great friends," he said, "if I gave you the chance." I nodded, and Austin looked at his bandaged feet. His eyes began to tear again, and his face turned red.

"I'm never going to the Olympics now, am I?" His tears rolled right off his face and onto the gauze. I sat with him until his mother arrived to take him to the hospital.

News had spread through the school at lightspeed, and by the time I got to class, everyone was buzzing about what had happened to Austin. It didn't take long for people to figure out that it wasn't just an accident. I was so blown away by the whole thing that I didn't even think about looking for Tyson. I was so spaced out by it that I didn't even realize until lunch that I was the prime suspect.

"I DIDN'T DO IT!" I screamed into Mr. Greene's face. I'd never screamed into a teacher's face before, but now I couldn't control myself. It was sixth period, just after lunch, and Greene had me called out of class to go to his office so he could accuse me of planting those rocks for Austin to fall on.

"I don't believe you!" he said, standing in front of his desk.

"I swear I didn't!"

"Oh, then it was just a coincidence that you were there when it happened?"

"Right!"

"And it was just a coincidence that you had a big fight with Austin yesterday?"

"It wasn't big!"

"And I suppose you're going to tell me you and your club had nothing to do with Vera's bike, or David's trumpet, or Drew's fish tank?"

"Right!"

"Come off it, Jared!" He pounded his desk. He was so sure he was right, it scared me. "It took me a while, but I found out exactly who's in your club. And you know what? Everyone in your club has a grudge against the very people who have been victims of this . . . this terrorism!"

"That's right," I said, "we're being framed!"

"Framed? By whom?"

"By Tyson McGaw!"

Greene wasn't ready for that. It took a few seconds for it to sink in, then he said, "If you think you're going to foist the blame on Tyson . . ."

"But it's true!"

"Tyson wouldn't do that, I know he wouldn't."

"But we have a witness," I said.

"Who?"

"Ralphy Sherman. He saw Tyson blow up the fish tank!"

"Yeah?" said Greene. "Ralphy Sherman also says that his mother had puppies. Do you expect me to believe a thing Ralphy Sherman says?"

"It's the truth! Why don't you bring Tyson in here, and accuse him like you're accusing me?"

"Because," said Greene, with nasty sarcasm in his voice, "Tyson didn't come to school today, Jared. Last I heard, he was being terrorized by a kid who beat him up and chased him out of school yesterday, screaming 'bed wetter' at the top of his lungs. Any idea who *that* was, Jared?" He looked at me as if I were a criminal. "You know, lots of people have spent years helping Tyson overcome a miserable childhood, and what you've done may have destroyed everything we've done to help him."

Greene gave me the evil eye for just a moment longer, then he sat down, pulled a gold pen out of his shirt, and began to write.

"I want you to take this note to your seventh-period teacher. It will excuse you from class. I'm also giving you a list of the classrooms in which each member of the Shadow Club can be found during seventh period. I want you to get them all out of class and bring them to my office so we can settle this once and for all." He handed me the note, just as the bell for seventh period rang. "And I think a talk with all of your parents tomorrow is in order as well."

I turned to leave.

"You have ten minutes. I'll be waiting for all of you. If you don't show, you'll be in even deeper trouble."

"Don't worry," I said. "You can trust me."

"Can I?"

"Of course."

Ten minutes later the Shadow Club was nowhere to be found. Greene must have scoured the school for us, but he didn't find us and wouldn't find us that day.

This was war now, and if we were going to prove our innocence, we had to treat it like a war. As soon as I had gotten everyone out of class, we split up and snuck out of school, all to meet in twenty minutes at Stonehenge.

Greene seemed to know an awful lot, and if he knew where Stonehenge was, then we'd all be in for it, so we just had to hope he didn't know.

Although it was cold and windy, with thick clouds blowing across the sky, for once my hands weren't cold; they were hot with anger. Anger at Tyson McGaw. If I never did anything else as president of the Shadow Club, I was going to make Tyson pay for what he had done.

The Inquisition

CHERYL AND I were the first at Stonehenge, since we ran all the way. One by one the rest began to trickle in: Darren, Abbie, Jason, and then O.P. Only Randall didn't show, and that made us worry. Generally speaking, Randall was the type of kid who might decide to go play video games instead, but maybe not—maybe he got caught. Maybe he was sitting in Greene's office right now. Maybe he'd talk and tell Greene where Stonehenge was.

"Would Randall give us away?" I asked Cheryl.

"Only if Greene grants him immunity" was her response. That sounded like Randall—he'd give us all away as long as he didn't get in trouble.

There was no fire in Stonehenge today; no fun stories and no good times. There were just six kids, standing, pacing, not sure of their next move.

"What do we do now?" asked Darren. "We're all on Greene's most-wanted list, and we're all in trouble. We all may be suspended from school!"

"Don't say that!" said Cheryl.

"It's true!" said Abbie. "Darren's right."

"Yeah," said Darren. "So what do we do now, Mr. and Mrs. Club President? Hmm?"

"I'm scared," said Jason. "I can't be suspended—heck, this is the first time I've ever cut class!"

"I can't afford to be suspended either! That kind of thing stays on your record forever," said O.P.

"So what do we do, Jared?"

"Yeah, what do we do?"

"There's only one thing we *can* do," I said. "We have to get Tyson. The only way we can clear ourselves is to make Tyson confess."

"I say we take the little creep and give him a taste of his own medicine!" said Abbie. Most everyone agreed.

"We don't even have to do that. Making him confess is all we have to do."

"Yeah, but we want revenge!" They all agreed on that. I have to admit, I wanted revenge, too—revenge for what he had done to my good friend Austin Pace.

"He'll be home with his aunt and uncle, or whatever they are. Our best chance is to tell them what Tyson's done. Unless they're as bad as Tyson, they'll believe us, and Tyson will be forced to confess."

"What if they don't believe us?" asked O.P.

"What if they're ax murderers like Ralphy Sherman says?" asked Jason.

"Shut up about that, OK?" I said. "They'll believe us—they have to." I looked at my watch. "If we're going to do it, we have to go now. It's almost three o'clock. Greene will be looking for us. Let's go."

I began to lead the way.

"Wait a minute," said Cheryl. "Randall won't be able to find us."

"Where could he have gone?" I asked.

"With Randall, there's no telling."

"You want to wait for him?"

"No," she said, "but I guess I have to. When you see Tyson, give him a good punch for me, OK?"

I turned and led the other four to Tyson's lighthouse.

We didn't talk much as we crossed through the woods and then the grassy field toward the lighthouse. It was getting colder, but it didn't bother me. Dark clouds were looming out over the ocean, but they were nothing compared to the storm clouds within each of our minds as we approached Tyson's front door.

As we got closer, I noticed that there was no car parked beside the house, as there had been the night I had spied on Tyson.

"Wait here," I said, and keeping low, I snuck around the house, looking into every window, leaving Tyson's window for last. Tyson was alone in the house, sitting at his desk, working on those ridiculous marionettes. This was perfect! Perfect! It was even better than I had hoped for.

I ran around to the living room window, which was open just a crack, carefully took off the screen, quietly worked the window wide open, then got the others.

"Hello, Tyson."

Tyson jumped about a mile when he heard me, sending the scissors and string in his hands flying across the room. His eyes went as wide as his beady little eyes could get. What a shocker that must have been, to see the five of us standing there, right at the threshold of his bedroom!

"Get up," I said calmly. Tyson looked at me, still shocked to see us there.

"I SAID, GET UP!"

"Get out of my house!" he said weakly.

I went up to him and pulled him out of his chair by his shirt, hearing it rip slightly.

"I'll call the police, and then you'll be in trouble!" he yelled. I ignored him.

"I like your room, Tyson," I said. "Nice view of the ocean you got here, isn't it? But what's that I smell, Tyson? What is it?"

"You better shut up!" he growled.

"Hey, Darren," I said. "Why don't you take the sheets off his bed? I think that's where the smell's coming from." Darren did what he was told and pulled back the blanket. The sheet underneath was clean, but when he pulled that away, there lay Tyson's rubber sheet for everyone to see. Tyson struggled, and I put him into a full nelson.

"Wow," said Jason. "You mean Tyson pees in his bed?"

"Oh, didn't you know that?" I said. "He does it every night. It's a wonder he doesn't have to wear diapers." Tyson struggled and I made the nelson tighter, pushing down on his head until he could barely move. "Did you know, Tyson, that Austin broke his ankle and he may never run again?" I forced the nelson even tighter. "I just thought you should know."

"I hate you!" he screamed. "I hate you!"

"The feeling's mutual!"

"You stupid Gopher," he said, and then something in my mind snapped. It was as if suddenly I wasn't me anymore—I was someone else—some*thing* else. Something evil. It was like I was possessed. I jerked Tyson around and took him out through the front door. He struggled all the way, kicking, knocking down lamps, leaving black footprints on the wall.

When I got him outside, I let him go, only to slug him full force in the face. He reeled and grunted, and I popped him one in the eye, then gave him an upper cut to the chin.

I couldn't stop! I was out of control. Then the rest of the club grabbed him, and held him back so he couldn't move. He couldn't even defend himself, and still I pounded away at him, thinking about Austin, and Vera, and Drew, and the rest.

I kept delivering punches to his stomach, as he tried to kick me away.

"Do I get a turn?" asked Jason.

"How about me?" asked Abbie. "For Vera!"

Finally I stopped. "Are you going to confess?" I growled at him, and in his pain he looked at me and said, "I don't confess to anything!"

I stepped right up to him, grabbing his shirt again, making sure I tugged it hard enough to rip it, and then, well, I'll never forget what I did next—I'll never believe it either; it will live on in my own nightmares.

I spat at him. Just like Randall had done, I spat at Tyson. I'm not proud of it; I'm pretty ashamed of it—all of it, if you must know—but that's what I did. Then I let go of him, and the club grabbed him, holding him back.

That dark cloud that had been in my mind was now in my blood, filling up my whole body. It was hatred—evil hatred—mixed with power, and together those two things are more dangerous than nitroglycerin. It filled me and took me over. At that moment none of us were the kids we had been before; we were monsters filled with one desire: destroy Tyson McGaw.

I stood there like Darth Vader, breathing the power. The power of club leader. I had Tyson McGaw in the palm of my hand, and all I could think to do with him was crush him—like I would crush a soda can.

"Take him to Stonehenge," I said.

"Yes, yes, to Stonehenge!" echoed the rest.

While they carried Tyson away, I called Jason over. "Go get all of his puppets," I said. "Tear down that clothesline and bring it along, and don't forget to bring the scissors."

At Stonehenge, while Jason played with the marionettes, the rest of us tied Tyson's arms to two separate trees with two pieces of clothesline. There was enough slack so that it wouldn't hurt, but he could barely move his arms.

Cheryl had vanished, leaving me alone as leader. She had probably gone off to look for Randall and would be back soon.

"You'll go to jail!" screamed Tyson, losing his voice. "All of you will! You'll see. When my uncle and Mr. Greene hear about it, you'll all be expelled from school! You'll see!"

I stood back, leaning against the wall of Stonehenge, letting the dark power flow through me. I watched as, by my command, the members of the Shadow Club yelled nasty things back at Tyson about him and his family, and pelted him with pinecones.

Jason, who had been examining the marionettes, turned to me and said, "Hey, these puppets are of us!" He was right. Now, looking closely at them, what I had first thought to be a coincidence was no coincidence at all. The entire Shadow Club was here, as well as some teachers, and other kids at school.

"What are these, voodoo dolls?" asked Abbie.

"You leave them alone!" said Tyson, spitting out words that I won't repeat. "They're mine!"

Jason looked at me, and I gave the signal. One by one, Jason cut the strings, and O.P. tore each of the marionettes into shreds, throwing them at Tyson's feet.

"Confess," said Darren, "and we'll stop," but Tyson didn't confess a thing. He was a hard nut to crack. In a few minutes there was a pile of little heads and arms and legs and string in front of Tyson. He tried to break free, but the ropes held.

"You're gonna pay for this," screamed Tyson. "Pay pay pay! All of you!"

"Confess," I said calmly, folding my arms, standing just out of his reach.

"I'll never confess to you!" he said.

The Shadow Club looked at me. Time for a new plan. I pointed to the ropes, snapped my fingers, and they ran to cut Tyson down.

"The beach!" I said, and I led the way as the rest carried him down toward the shore.

We hauled Tyson down the rocks to the small cove closest to Stonehenge, just below where Cheryl and I had our first kiss. The cove was hidden, with no homes anywhere nearby, so no one could catch us. It was close to 4:30

when we got there, but it seemed even later, because those black clouds over the ocean were closer now, churning up the sea.

We let Tyson go, but formed a semicircle in front of him. With the ocean right behind him, there was nowhere he could run.

"Leave me alone!" he whined. "Let me go home! My aunt and uncle will be home soon, and they'll be looking for me! You're gonna be in so much trouble!"

"We'll let you go home as soon as you confess!" I said. "What's so hard about that?"

"I don't have anything to confess, gopher brain!"

"You're lying," said O.P., "and I'm not going to be suspended from school because of what *you* did!" And with that we began to move closer to him. Tyson backed away until his dirty, torn tennis shoes were being washed over by the icy October sea.

"Stop!" he said. "You're all dead meat! All of you!" We got closer and he backed away farther.

"What are you going to do to me?" he asked, suddenly not as angry as he was frightened.

"Nothing," I said, "if you confess."

By now, the waves were crashing at his knees and at our feet, but we didn't care how wet we got, as long as we forced Tyson to admit the pranks he had pulled.

"It's cold . . ." Tyson backed away a bit more. The water

was now breaking at his waist and at our knees, then in one last mercy cry he said, "I can't swim . . ."

When I heard that, I smiled a dark, evil smile, and moved closer. If Tyson couldn't swim, then he would *have* to confess. Either that or learn to swim real quick!

That's when I heard Cheryl calling from far away. "Jared!" I looked up; she was on the cliff. "Jared, come here," she called.

"I'm busy! You come down here!"

"It's an emergency!"

"So is this!"

"No," she said, "I mean a *real* emergency."

Figuring that Cheryl had to have the worst timing in the world, I reluctantly left. "You're in charge," I told Darren. "I want a confession from him by the time I get back."

And I left them—four kids, and one rough sea, to do battle against Tyson McGaw.

What Happened to Randall

A S I HAD guessed, Cheryl had left Stonehenge to find her brother, but when she had arrived at home, she hadn't found Randall there. Instead, she had found a note that said to call her parents at a strange number, which turned out to be the hospital. Randall was in the hospital and Cheryl didn't know why. Her parents weren't entirely sure yet either, but whatever it was, they had been pretty stressed out about it, and so was Cheryl.

They told her to wait at home until she heard from them again, but Cheryl's not the type to sit at home waiting.

"Do you think your mom's home by now?" she asked me.

"Probably."

"Good. I need a ride to the hospital."

We ran all the way to my house. My mom had just gotten home from work, and when she heard about Randall, she hurried us off into the car and took us to the hospital.

The hospital was big and white, like all hospitals in

the world seem to be, and it smelled like a hospital. I hated that smell; it reminded me of the time I had my tonsils out.

Paul, Cheryl's stepdad, met us in the lobby, surprised, but not upset, to see us.

"It's OK," he said. "It's not as bad as we first thought. He didn't hit his head or anything. They think he might have fractured his hip though."

"Oh no!" said my mother, "Poor Randall!"

"What happened?" I asked.

"Near as I can tell, he was playing basketball in some friend's backyard, went for a shot, took a bad fall, and came down hard on the cement. I don't know the whole story."

Cheryl and I looked at each other, but said nothing. Ten minutes later, Randall was wheeled out of X ray. He looked awful. He had been given painkillers and barely seemed to be able to move on that gurney. I had a bad feeling about this—even worse than the feeling I had when I realized Austin was about to plow into those rocks.

We all followed as Randall was wheeled into a room. The doctor examined him again and then left with his parents to examine the X rays. When my mother stepped out, we were left alone with Randall.

"Tell us what happened, Randy," Cheryl said.

"I broke my hip," he said groggily.

"We know," said Cheryl. "Paul said you were playing basketball? Where was it?"

Randall closed his eyes and took a deep breath. "Eric Kilfoil's," he said, "and I wasn't playing basketball."

Cheryl and I looked at each other in disbelief, and that's when I realized that the entire bottom had just dropped out of the Shadow Club.

"Tell us what happened, if you can," asked Cheryl. Slowly, quietly, Randall told us. He told us how he went over to Eric's house after he snuck out of school, instead of coming to Stonehenge. He told us that he had been planning it for days, and he knew no one was home. He told us how he climbed onto the roof of Eric's garage, carrying tools to take down Eric's backboard and hoop and steal it. Halfway through unscrewing the thing, however, the backboard fell without warning. Randall lost his balance, and plunged to the ground. "I would still be there if the neighbors hadn't heard me yelling," he said.

"Why did you do it?" asked Cheryl. Neither of us knew that Randall could do such a thing. Sure, he was a brat, but planning to steal something like that . . . Well, it made us both wonder what else he might have done.

"I did it for Darren," he said. "Because Darren's my friend, and he doesn't deserve to be treated the way Eric treats him. I just wanted to get Eric back for Darren, that's all."

"Does Darren know you did this?" I asked.

"No."

I swallowed and asked the question that I was afraid to hear the answer to. "Randall . . . did you pull all those other pranks, too?"

"No!" he said, grimacing from the pain in his side. "I swear, I only pulled this one! Only this one! Tyson pulled the rest!"

Cheryl looked away from me when I turned to her, and finally the last piece of the puzzle snapped into place. It fit so well that I knew I was right. I had to be. I knew the truth, and it was so ugly that I was afraid to accept it. It was uglier and more horrible than anything we could have imagined.

"Cheryl, can I talk to you?"

"Sure." Cheryl gave Randall a kiss on his forehead, and even in his sedated state, he was able to lift his hand and wipe it off. We stepped out into the hall.

"Do you think Tyson pulled all the rest of the tricks, like Randall said?" I asked straight out.

"Of course," she said.

"What about Austin?" I asked. "Did Tyson do that?"

"I guess." Cheryl shrugged, and looked away from me— and that wasn't right; Cheryl doesn't look away like that. Not unless she knows something that she doesn't want to tell.

It was time for me to pull a bluff. It was a mean, nasty

bluff to pull on Cheryl, but I had to do it. Things were way out of hand, and if what I suspected was true, we were all in more trouble than humanly possible. I had to trick Cheryl if I was going to find out the truth.

"You're lying!" I said right to her face.

"What?"

"I know he didn't do it!" I said. "You did it."

That lawyer look came over her face—the look she had whenever she was about to argue somebody down into the ground.

"How dare you accuse me of something like that, Jared Mercer! I thought we trusted each other!"

"We do, but you did it."

"You don't have proof of that!"

"Yes I do," I lied. "I saw you. I saw you planting the stones, I just didn't want to say anything until now. I saw you, Cheryl!"

My heart sort of locked up for a while; I would swear I was having a heart attack or something. If I was wrong, then this little lie may have just ripped apart my lifelong friendship with Cheryl. If I was right, then it would be even worse. Either way, we were going to lose.

Cheryl gave me the lawyer look for a while longer, but the anger faded from her face.

"You should have said something before," she said. "That wasn't fair." She looked away from me for a moment, then looked back. "All right, I did do it," she said. I bit my tongue and tried hard not to react. "I did it for you," she said. "I didn't mean for him to get so hurt. I just wanted to scratch him up a bit so that you'd get to run in the District Olympics like you wanted to."

For a split second I had the nauseous feeling that this wasn't Cheryl. This was some vile, sickening creature that had taken Cheryl's form, but was still dark and evil inside. Then the feeling passed and I realized that this was Cheryl through and through—and what I saw in her was just a reflection of myself. That was the worst thought of all. It was like a disease that took root in both of us—all of us—the moment we started the club, and was growing ever since.

"It's what you wanted!" she said. "Yesterday you said that you wished Austin was hurt! You told me so!"

She was right; I had told her that. It was my fault as much as hers. "What about the other tricks, Cheryl?"

"I didn't do them, honest, I swear. I only pulled that one. Only that one! Tyson pulled the rest!"

It was just as I thought—no doubt about it. At first I figured that Tyson framing us would be the worst thing that could happen. This was even worse. I began to back away.

"I'm sorry!" she said. "Don't look at me like that. I just wanted to help you! I'm sorry!"

I couldn't face her; not right then. I didn't know if I

could ever face her again—much less hold her hand, or kiss her. I didn't want to be near her, so I turned and ran.

"Jared . . . !" she called after me, but I didn't stop. I could hear that she was already crying as she called my name. I had never seen her cry, and I guessed I wouldn't now, because I didn't look back.

I burst into the lobby, passing my confused mother on my way out of the hospital. As I raced through the front door into the cold evening, never slowing down, the full meaning of my discovery began to hit home.

Greene was right!

Greene was right all along, about everything. The truth was that the Shadow Club *did* pull all of the pranks—*all* of them, but we didn't even know it! Cheryl hit Austin for me, Randall hit Eric for Darren, Jason probably blew up the fish tank for Randall, and the amazing thing about it was that everyone did it secretly; no one knew what the others were up to, and we were all convinced that Tyson had done all the rest.

What had I done? Tyson was the most innocent of us all!

I raced down the road, never slowing my pace. My gopher shirt was drenched in sweat by the time I had run the three miles to the ocean. As I approached the cliff, it occurred to me that Greene and Tyson were right about one more thing: the Shadow Club wasn't a club at all; it was a gang. Sure, we didn't have guns or switchblades, but we caused plenty of damage just the same. Hate doesn't need a weapon.

We were a gang, and I was a bully. A gang leader.

The ocean was rough, and the storm clouds were almost overhead. It was 6:00 and the sun had set long ago. I searched the small strip of beach, but neither Tyson nor the Shadow Club was anywhere in sight. I headed for Stonehenge.

I burst through the trees and jumped down into the pit, half expecting nobody to be there, but, nearly hidden in the shadows, sat the four other members of the club, all shivering and soaking wet with seawater. They all had looks on their faces somewhere between terror and shock.

"Where's Tyson?" I asked, terrified myself of what they might tell me.

No one answered me for a while, then Darren looked up at me and spoke like a child.

"Jared . . . I think we did something real bad . . ."

I sat down with them. I didn't want to hear this, but I knew I had to. "We all did something real bad," I said, leaning against the stone wall, feeling the wind blow across my cold, sweaty shirt.

Darren looked down, and no one said anything. In that long silence a thought came to me. I suddenly realized that Hell wasn't a place filled with fire and smoke—Hell was cold, wet, and lonely. Hell was the dead stone foundation of an old building in the woods.

I pulled my knees to my chest, shivering as I felt the cold stone behind me, then laid my head in my hands, and said, "Tell me what happened to Tyson."

The Confession

WHEN YOU LEFT," began Darren, "we kept walking Tyson deeper and deeper into the water. He kept cursing and yelling like he always does, but then, I don't know, I guess he started getting really scared. A big wave crashed into his back, and he nearly went under. When he got his balance back, he starts begging, 'Please,' he says, 'please, I'll do anything you want, just let me out of the water.'

"We all told him we wouldn't let him out until he confessed—then an even bigger wave breaks right behind him, and knocks him down, washing him toward us. I caught him. He was coughing and sputtering, and he says, 'I'll confess, I'll confess anything. Let me go home!'"

That's where Darren stopped.

"So, what happened?" I asked. They all looked at me. "Well? Tell me!"

"He confessed," said Abbie.

"What?"

"He confessed, but not to the pranks." Abbie brushed her wet hair out of her face. "He said he didn't do the pranks, so he couldn't confess to that."

"Go on, what did he confess?"

They all looked at me, then looked at each other, then looked down.

"The fires," said Jason. It took a few seconds to sink in. Jason continued. "He told us that he set all the school fires. He burned down the gym last year and set all the smaller fires. He set the cafeteria fire last month, too."

"Why?"

"He's a pyromaniac," said O.P. "That's what I figure. He gets off on setting fires."

"Oh, God!" I buried my head in my hands, remembering how we all watched as the gym burned down last year. Yet somehow I couldn't hate Tyson anymore. I couldn't hate anyone for anything. Instead I felt sorry for him. Those dark, empty eyes weren't empty at all; there was fire buried in them that nobody saw. I wondered if Greene even knew about it.

"There's more," said Darren. "This is the bad part." He leaned his head back. I could tell by his voice that he was crying a little. "When he told us about the fires," continued Darren, "I got real crazy. I . . . I started to dunk his head in the water over and over again . . ."

"Oh, no!" I yelled. "How could you do that?"

"I don't know! I just started thinking about that fireman they carried out of the gym last year, and about all the people that could have been killed, and if you were there you would have done the same thing, 'cause you were acting just as crazy as me!"

A shiver began in my back, working its way up to my head. Darren was right, I probably would have done it.

"We all helped," said Jason. "We all kept pushing him in the water, and he kept yelling, then gasping, then he didn't make any noises at all."

"We were gonna stop," added O.P., "but a gigantic wave hit all of us. We were all knocked down, and by the time we got our balance and stood up, Tyson wasn't there."

I stared at them in disbelief.

"That's when the craziness sort of just went away," said Darren, "and we all realized what we had done. We searched and searched the water, but we couldn't find Tyson. It seemed like we were searching for ten minutes . . . and then, another wave rolled in, and we saw him tossed over in the crest, facedown. We all swam out to him and dragged him back to shore. It was scary, Jared—he was so limp and so heavy."

"I resuscitated him," said O.P. "I didn't even know if I was doing it right, but I must have been, 'cause it worked. He coughed up water and just kept coughing, so we rolled him onto his side.

"He was really dazed," continued Darren. "I don't know if he was even completely conscious at first, but then a minute later, he stumbles up, and begins to run away."

"He threw a rock at us," said Abbie. "It nearly hit Darren in the head."

"Do you blame him?" I asked.

"No," said Jason. "Anyway, he ran up the way we came, coughing, cursing, and screaming, 'I'll show you! I'll show you!' That was the last we saw of him."

So that was it. "What a mess," I said, figuring that to be the biggest understatement of my life.

"There's one more thing," said Darren. "We came back here to wait for you on account of we were afraid to go home, since Greene had probably called all our parents. While we sat here waiting we found something out." Darren looked down—nobody could look me in the face.

"Tyson . . . didn't . . . pull . . . the pranks," said Darren. He stopped for a while, then said, "I cut Vera's brakes," and Abbie said, "I poured paint in Eric's locker," and O.P. said, "I put David's trumpet behind the bus," and Jason said, "I put the blockbuster in the fish tank—I didn't mean to blow it up. I also hid the camera in Tommy Nickols' locker."

"We figured Cheryl or Randall put the rocks down for Austin," said Darren.

"Cheryl did," I said.

"Thought so," said Darren.

"What did you do?" asked O.P.

I thought about it. "I did the worst thing of all," I said. "It was my idea to start pulling pranks to begin with."

We sat there for the longest time, cold and wet, afraid to go anywhere.

"So what do we do now?" asked Abbie. "What happens when we get home? What happens tomorrow? What happens at school on Monday?"

"Whatever happens to us happens. We deserve it. Anyway, let's not think about any of that now." I stood up. "I'm going to Tyson's house," I said, "to start . . . unscrewing things up, and apologize."

"How do you apologize for nearly killing someone?" asked O.P.

"I don't know," I said. "I've never almost killed someone before."

One by one they all stood to follow me, and we walked out of Stonehenge together, but as we did I noticed something and knelt down beside it. It was the pile of marionette heads, arms, legs, and bodies torn to bits. He must have spent hours on each one. Now they were beyond repair.

"Why do you think he made those?" asked Abbie.

"I think I know," said Jason. "He doesn't have any friends. He had to make up friends of his own."

"We were all in his collection," I said. "I guess we should have been flattered." I stood and led the way to Tyson's house.

Fire and Water

SOMETHING WAS WRONG at the lighthouse. There were lights in the windows, but they were the wrong color, and they flickered.

Darren realized it first. "It's on fire!" he said, and we ran toward it. "Tyson set the place on fire!"

The front door was wide open, just as we had left it, and Tyson's aunt and uncle were still not home. As I peered in, I could see flames eating up the living room. There wasn't much time to think, or to do much of anything, but one thought did make its way to my brain. If Tyson was in there, and he died, it would be my fault, because we pushed him to do it. I knew that I couldn't live with that; I couldn't live with it for one single day!

I ran through the front door, as the rest of the club screamed for me to stop.

Inside, it didn't seem as bad as it had looked from the outside. The drapes were on fire, the furniture and part of the floor, too, but I could make my way around easily, if I held my breath. I ran down the hall that was just beginning to catch fire, but when I looked into Tyson's room I had to turn away—the fire was everywhere. I couldn't see a thing, and could feel the heat all around me! There was no way I could get near the room.

Fire moves faster than most people probably think it does. When I turned around, the hallway was blocked off by flames, so I turned and ran through a door, finding myself in the kitchen. It was amazing, but nothing in the kitchen was on fire yet. I closed the door behind me.

That's when I began to get scared. Really scared. It just came over me, nearly making me pass out. Smoke filled the room, and I could hear the rumble of the flames eating up the walls around me. There were no windows in the small kitchen, and only one other door. I ran to open it.

It was locked.

Turning the knob, I pushed on it again and again, but it wouldn't budge. I was trapped! I heard the television explode in the living room, and I realized that coming into this burning house was the biggest mistake I had ever made. That's when I did it.

I wet my pants.

That's right, I wet my pants, and I'm not ashamed of it either! I was on the verge of frying to death! No human being can stand that stress.

Anyway, I didn't realize it right away; I was too

busy kicking at the door. Then for no particular reason, I turned the knob and pulled rather than pushed. The door opened.

How stupid! I thought to myself. How stupid it would be if I died because I was too much of an idiot to pull the door instead of push it!

I closed the door behind me and found myself in a round room, standing before an old wooden spiral staircase. I was inside the base of the lighthouse.

Behind me the roar of the flames got loud, and I knew that the kitchen was history; I had gotten out just in time. Ahead of me lay the spiral staircase, no windows or doors, and so up I went.

At the top of the stairs, I found myself inside a dirty glass booth, the light cage, I think it's called. In the center of the round booth was the old light that hadn't been used for dozens of years.

I saw him right away. Tyson sat between the light cage and the railing that ran around it, clutching something in his hands and rocking back and forth. He saw me right away, too. I stepped out of the light cage, and onto the ledge. He looked up at me. His eyes were red from tears; my eyes were red from smoke. He picked something up that lay next to him—a broken piece of brick—and he hurled it at me. It hit me in the shoulder. I tried not to feel it.

"Go away!" he said through his tears. "Just go away!" He

threw something else—this time a shard of thick glass. I ducked and it went over the rail.

"I hate you!" he screamed. "Hate-you-hate-you-hate-you! I wish you were dead! I wish . . . I wish you were never born!"

I moved slowly in on him, and he leaned away, still clutching whatever it was he was clutching. "Tyson," I said, "the fire's almost here! We've got to figure out a way down!"

"No. I'm staying. You can jump for all I care."

"Tyson, I'm trying to help you!"

"Yeah, sure you are."

I held out my hand to him, and he turned away. "No!" he screamed, holding the thing he was holding far away from me. "No! You're not taking this, too!" He stood and ran around the ledge and I ran after him, going in circles until I finally caught him. He turned and threw it at me, hitting me in the forehead. I tried not to feel it.

"Take it!" he screamed. "Take it, I don't care. I don't care, I don't care . . ." He fell to his knees, crying, and rocking back and forth, and I looked at what he had been holding. It was the picture of him and his parents—the one thing he had saved from his room before setting it on fire. I knelt beside him. He was crying harder than ever now.

"Why are you doing this to me?" he mumbled. "Why? Why? Why? You never used to bother me like the other kids in school did. Now you're the worst. Well, I don't care," he said. "When the fire gets here, it won't matter. Then every-one'll be sorry."

"I already am sorry, Tyson." Tyson just sobbed and sobbed. He wasn't even fighting me off anymore. He just sobbed and rocked back and forth.

I felt funny about it, but I put my arm around him, like he was my kid or something. He didn't stop crying. "I'm your friend now, Tyson. I'll always be your friend. I've never been so wrong about anybody in my entire life, and I'll make it up to you."

"I didn't pull those pranks," he mumbled.

"I know. I was wrong." We sat there for a moment, and then I looked down at myself. "Look at me," I said. "I pissed in my pants!" He looked at my pants, then up at me, and for a second I thought I saw a smile there beneath the tears. I smiled at him. "Welcome to the club, right?" I said.

He shrugged.

"Sure. We can call it the Pee-Pee Club!"

He didn't say anything.

"C'mon," I said, "it'll be a real pisser!"

And at that, he laughed. It was short, but at least he laughed.

There was a light in the lighthouse, but it wasn't the kind of light you'd want to see—the lighthouse base was on fire. Whatever wood was down there had caught and was be-ing eaten up. Smoke started to pour out of the light cage.

"We'd better get out of here," I said, helping Tyson up.

"You go," he said. "I want to stay."

"Don't be dumb." I looked over the railing. "How far down is it?"

"Pretty far," said Tyson.

It seemed a long way down to the ground, but flames were already licking up inside the light cage. The flames from the house made it impossible to jump on any side, except for the side facing the sea, and so, as the flames began to reach out of the light cage, Tyson climbed over the railing. I didn't just yet. I ran around to the other side of the light cage, picked up Tyson's picture, smashed the glass, and took out the photo.

Tyson was still clinging to the ledge when I got back. I climbed over to the other side, and we sort of just stood there for a while, as the fire became fiercer. I thought of the time I was on a five-meter high board. I had stood there at the edge, looking over for a good ten minutes before I got the nerve to jump. We couldn't do that now.

"On the count of three," I said. "One . . . two . . . three!" We both let go without looking down, then hit the side and slid down the slope of the lighthouse. The stone was hot from the fire inside. We hit the bushes beside the lighthouse hard, but they were dense enough to break our fall. Still, we didn't stop, because the bushes sloped off quickly to the rocks above the ocean. We kept rolling, then suddenly I found myself rolling down rocks. The cliff wasn't too steep, but the rocks sure were jagged. Finally we stopped, just above the ocean. Tyson, who was falling backward, probably would have smashed his head if he hadn't landed on me first.

I looked up, and the lighthouse seemed amazingly far away. It was hard to believe we had tumbled all this way in such a short time.

It was high tide, the rocks were wet and slippery, the wind felt like a hurricane, and the waves kept hitting below, shooting water up through the crevices like a whale's blow-hole. There was no way we could climb back up, but the storm offshore was churning up the sea so much, it seemed the ocean was no escape either. The waves were at least ten feet high now.

Another wave came in, and this one lifted us both up and smashed us down against the rocks again, sending foam flying in all directions.

"Ow!" I yelled. That one hurt! These were the types of waves that turned boulders into sand, and we would be dust if we sat there much longer.

Up above, there was an explosion.

"Watch out!" said Tyson. The entire light cage had shattered, sending shards of heavy glass down in our direction. "Duck!"

Big splinters of glass and burning wood landed all around. Up above, the frame of the house fell, and the burning beams seemed about ready to come toppling down the rocks toward us. Our only chance was to get off the rocks, and make our way to the beach.

"But I can't swim!" said Tyson.

"I know," I said as I saw a wave—the darkest, meanest-looking one yet—looming in front of us, blocking out the rest of the ocean. "I can swim, though. Hold on to me!" I said. "I won't let you go."

Before we had time to figure out how we were going to work this, the wave was upon us. Tyson grabbed me around the waist, and we were underwater. The wave rolled us, dragging us across the rocks, then dragging us back, spinning us every which way around until I couldn't tell which way was up.

When my head broke the surface, we were off the rocks and out in the icy open sea, a hundred long yards from the beach. I kicked off my shoes, and with Tyson sputtering, coughing, and gagging, I began to swim toward shore, with him holding on to my belt for his life. At that moment I would have given anything in the world to have been Drew Landers, or even Randall; two strong swimmers who could handle this better than I could.

Tyson was panicking, nearly pulling me under each time a wave hit us, but somehow we kept our heads above water. My arms could barely stretch away from my body to pull the water, but my legs were strong from track. I kept kicking, counting each kick, and praying, which I never seemed to do enough of unless I thought I was going to die. All we needed was a riptide to drag us out into the sea, and we'd never be seen again. I began to wonder if there were any sharks around here. There were stories about people who got eaten by sharks nearby, and Ralphy Sherman says—well, to hell with what Ralphy Sherman says.

A wave broke around us, carried us over the crest, and smashed us down on the shells—but that was all right, because it was land! When we came up, Tyson was still gagging. I grabbed his hand, got my balance, and limped with him to shore. The water was so cold that the second I stood, my legs cramped into knots. I could barely move, so as soon as we reached the beach, we collapsed on the wet sand.

"I've got to . . . I've got to teach you to swim!" I said to Tyson. "So the next time this happens . . ." I thought about that and began to laugh. I coughed, laughed, choked, and cried all at the same time.

On the other side of the rocks, we could hear sirens. The firemen had finally arrived, but there wasn't much to put out—the entire house had fallen over, tumbling down into the ocean. All that remained was the shell of the lighthouse, looking like some short, pudgy smokestack. Somewhere up there stood the rest of the Shadow Club, probably thinking we were both dead. What a surprise they were in for!

"Hey, Tyson," I said. He turned to me. "Here." I reached

into my back zippered pocket and took out a folded photograph, handing it to him. "I figured you'd want this."

Tyson took it, rolled over, and looked at it, while I looked over his shoulder. His parents didn't look all that greasy. Neither did he, back then.

"It's the only picture I have of my parents," he said.

"What happened to them?" I asked.

"They died when I was seven," he said, and then he added, ". . . in a fire."

He kept staring at that photo. It was wet and faded, but it was all he had.

As I lay there in the cold, waiting for my muscles to uncramp, a dumb thought came to mind. Now that I was soaking wet, I realized that no one would ever know that I had wet my pants. I never did tell anyone about it—not my parents, not Cheryl, not anyone. It was a secret between Tyson and me.

The Burning of the Charter

THE SUN ROSE the next morning.

All night long, even after they had released me from the hospital, I kind of had the funny feeling like it wouldn't—or if it did, the clouds would be so dark, the day would still seem like night.

But the sun rose, and the sky was clear. I ducked under the covers to block out the light, and coughed—I was still coughing from the smoke.

My father came into the room and pulled the covers off my head. "Get yourself dressed," he said coldly. I had never heard him use that tone of voice with me. It was as if he were talking to a stranger. Maybe he was.

The night before had been filled with such confusion, neither of my parents was sure what was going on. But now my watch read 11:15 A.M. I knew that by now they would have found out about the club, and about what we had done.

"I'm in lots of trouble, aren't I?" I mumbled, knowing full well that no matter how much deep water I was in, I deserved every ounce of it.

"Trouble, Jared?" said my father, with a bitter smile that wasn't really a smile at all. "Trouble's not the word for it. Get up. We're taking a trip to Vice Principal Greene's house." My dad didn't say much else about it; neither did my mom. They're not the lecturing type. Still, I'll never forget that icy tone of disappointment in my dad's voice when he said, "I never thought I'd see my son in a gang."

So we all confessed. You must have seen it in the papers:

LOCAL KIDS TERRORIZE SCHOOL AND BURN HOUSE

Oh, it was a big deal. Everyone knows about it. Everyone knows that I was the leader. But nobody knows the whole story. Not yet anyway. Sure, we all confessed to Mr. Greene, and we all got suspended, and now we have to pay for what we did. But when he asked us why we did it, no one could tell him. We all just looked down. It was the way he treated us—like criminals—lying, cheating, stealing criminals. It was as if, in his eyes, we weren't kids anymore. We weren't people. And so we just couldn't talk to him about it, you know?

He still doesn't know that there was one more meeting of the Shadow Club—if you can call it a meeting. It was on Monday, the first day of a two-week suspension, which could have been an all-out expulsion if our parents hadn't all been such pillars of the community.

I didn't want to go. To me the Shadow Club had died a much-deserved death in the fire. Cheryl called the meeting. I couldn't say as I wanted to see her just yet either, but she begged, and so I went. I didn't go alone, though. I brought Tyson with me.

Tyson was living in a hotel with his aunt and uncle, who, as we all had guessed, were really foster parents. No one was sure whether Tyson burned down the house or the Shadow Club did. Tyson confessed, but I said it was the club. I wasn't about to let Tyson take the rap alone.

The two of us snuck away and walked together through the woods to Stonehenge. He didn't talk much. Neither did I. I guess it must have been awfully confusing to be Tyson McGaw just then. First I terrorize him, and then I ask him to come back to the scene of the crime. I don't know why he came when I asked him. Maybe it was because I *did* ask him. But whatever the reason, I was glad that he came.

As we neared Stonehenge, I could already see the smoke from the fire, but when I got closer I could see only one person down in the pit. Cheryl. She looked up at me for a few moments. I didn't step down just yet.

"Where's everyone else?" I asked.

"Not here yet. Hi, Tyson. Why don't you both come down?"

Reluctantly, I stepped down into the pit, and Tyson followed. I sat across the fire from Cheryl. "So, what is it you want?" I asked.

"Let's wait till they all get here," she said.

"Fine."

And so we waited, and waited, and waited. We waited for almost an hour.

No one else showed.

When the fire started to go out, I said, "Did you really expect anyone to come?"

She shook her head. "Too much to hope for, huh?" She looked at Tyson, and Tyson looked away, so she turned back to me. "I have a list here. I've figured out how much money each of us has to pay in damages, except for Tyson's house, of course."

I stood up. "Money?" I yelled. "How about Austin? What do we use to pay him back? Do we buy him new feet?"

Cheryl looked down. "I'm just as sorry about everything as you are," she said. Then she added, "You know, you didn't have to take the blame for what I did to Austin."

"I wanted to!" I said. "It was my fault as much as it was yours."

"Greene wants to give you a youth-delinquent card, doesn't he?" she asked.

"Of course he does. He's been storing them up, just waiting for the chance to use them."

"He won't," said Tyson. We both turned to him. "You gotta be a repeat offender to get one. I don't even have one." He shrugged and smiled. To see a smile from Tyson in this whole situation was a strange thing. I couldn't figure him out. I didn't know how he could like me after what I had caused, but the fact that he did like me made me want to be his friend. It made me want to trust him.

"I called the meeting so we could take care of *this* once and for all." Cheryl reached into her folder and took out the Shadow Club Charter, with everyone's signature on it. We had signed it less than two months ago, but it seemed like another lifetime. Cheryl looked at the charter for a moment, then handed it to Tyson. "You may have the honors."

Tyson looked at it, then at me. I nodded. Tyson shrugged and folded the paper into a plane, then sent it sailing into the fire. The dying flames leapt up and pulled the plane down. Its wings blackened and shriveled, until a breeze caught the fragile ashes that remained, and tore them apart.

"I hereby declare the Shadow Club dissolved, and the charter to be null and void throughout eternity," said Cheryl.

"Amen," I said, and doused the fire. When I was done, I saw Cheryl looking around Stonehenge. There were candy wrappers, Coke cans, and potato chip bags to mark the fact that we had been there all these weeks.

"Maybe this place is haunted," she said. "Maybe we were all possessed by some evil spirit or something."

"Naah," I said. "I think we just got possessed by ourselves."

Tyson was already climbing out of the pit. I was about to follow, when Cheryl stopped me.

"Jared?"

I turned to her. "Yeah?"

It took a while for her to ask her question, and because it took so long, I knew what the question was going to be.

"Jared . . . are we still . . . together?"

I thought about that for a second. "I don't know."

The answer didn't make her very happy. She looked down. "I know the real question," she said. "Are we still friends? That's the real question," she said in a voice that was almost a whisper.

I didn't answer for a long time. "I don't know," I said softly. "Ask me again next week."

"I see," she said quietly, and backed away. She had always been so tough, but now I could almost see her falling apart inside.

"No," I said, moving closer to her. "I mean *really* ask me again next week. Right now I'm not even my own friend." I kissed her. Whatever the kiss meant, we'd have to wait to find out. We both seemed to feel a little better, though.

At the lip of Stonehenge, Tyson was kneeling down, trying to piece together his mutilated marionettes. He turned to me as we came out of the pit and said, "Couldn't you have left a single one? It'll take years to make more!"

"What do you need them for? Now you've got the real

thing!" I helped him up, and for the first time since the day I knocked him out of the phone booth, I looked in his eyes. They were dark and deep, just as always. There was a lot of heavy stuff going on down there; deep, dark memories that no kid should have. Maybe I'd find out about them someday, maybe not, but one thing was certain; whatever was in those eyes, I wasn't afraid of it anymore. He kept staring at me, probably because I was staring at him. I wondered what it was he saw in *my* eyes.

"Things are gonna be rough for a while, Tyson," I said, "for all of us."

"It's OK," he said, "I'm used to that." And he smiled, a real, full smile, and it made both Cheryl and me feel much better about things. It sort of made us realize that it was all gonna pass, and things were gonna be OK—that is, if we all worked hard enough to make it OK.

Cheryl and I turned and took one last look down into the shadowy pit of Stonehenge. We both knew we wouldn't come back here again. It was a place from our past. Like the tree house.

Tyson was waiting for us, and so we left, turning our backs on Stonehenge forever.

Epilogue

THAT WAS YESTERDAY. I think Cheryl needs to think things over, just like me. I guess you might call this a trial separation for us, and those don't always end in divorce, you know.

Anyway, tomorrow Cheryl's going to see a psychologist, too. Just to talk. I guess it works, because after this, I realize how much I want to talk about it, and tell everyone how it happened.

And I know who has to hear it next:

Austin.

Austin's parents might not let me in the house, and maybe he'll hate me for all eternity. But maybe after a long time he'll see how sorry I really am, and he'll forgive me. I mean, if Tyson can forgive me, anything's possible.

And Tyson won't be sorry he did, either. I might be the second-best runner, but from now on I'm gonna be the best friend either of them ever had. And when it comes right down to it, as long as I'm the best friend I can be, who cares what I'm second-best at?